CONCERTO FOR FEAR

1940s private detective Red Benton puts his ingenuity and charm to work in two stories of mystery and murder. *Concerto for Fear* features a murderous piano and a seemingly cursed new piece of music with a deadly low G. And in *Death Flows Down River*, two corpses are fished out of the water with curious neat incisions in their abdomens — and Red makes what turns out to be perhaps the worst mistake of his career when he sends an innocent woman on what he thinks is a routine investigation . . .

NORMAN FIRTH

$\blacklozenge$

CONCERTO
FOR FEAR

Complete and Unabridged

LINFORD
Leicester

First published in Great Britain

First Linford Edition
published 2014

A catalogue record for this book is available
from the British Library.

ISBN 978–1–4448–2085–0

Published by
F. A. Thorpe (Publishing)
Anstey, Leicestershire

Set by Words & Graphics Ltd.
Anstey, Leicestershire
Printed and bound in Great Britain by
T. J. International Ltd., Padstow, Cornwall

This book is printed on acid-free paper

Concerto for Fear

1

'Lady to see youse, Borss,' grunted 'Happy' Harringay, appearing in the doorway of the inner office.

Red Benton, private detective extraordinaire, swung his grey-clad legs lazily onto his desk, lit a cigarette and regarded his stumpy assistant without interest. 'How does she look?' he drawled.

'She's a wow, Borss — got everything, this dame. You wanta see her?' replied Happy enthusiastically. As Red hesitated, he added: 'She's de bee's knees, I tell ya.'

'All right, Happy, I'll take your word — shoot her in!'

Happy Harringay vanished from the doorway, to be replaced by a woman. Red regarded her with interest and allowed himself a low whistle. She was class all right — Park Lane written all over her, from the top of her ridiculous hat to the tips of her exclusive shoes. She was dressed in a neat, form-fitting black costume which did things for her figure, and sheer stockings. Her features were the features of a girl who was used to getting her own way — but at the moment they wore a worried expression. One black-gloved hand patted the golden hair at the nape of her neck into place, as she saw Red looking at her. Then she came forward with a slinky movement, right to the desk, and looked down at him.

'Mister Benton?' she asked in a rich, honey-like voice.

Red made no effort to get up from the reclining position. He merely nodded, blew a cloud of smoke in her direction, then stubbed out his cigarette. 'Sit down — find yourself a chair,' he said agreeably. 'And state what's on your mind.'

The girl looked at him, a little taken aback. 'You — you *are* Mister Benton, aren't you?'

'If I'm not, I've got no right in this office,' he told her.

'The detective?' she asked, determined to get things clear.

Red nodded. 'Red Benton, Investigations, at your service,' he informed her

4

patiently. Certainly she was justified in being a little surprised. For Red Benton bore no resemblance whatever to the popular conception of a noted private investigator. He was slight and lean, and at the moment his entire body was relaxed in a sprawling attitude. His grey-green eyes peered at her curiously, and above them his tousled shock of carroty hair (by which he had been given the nickname of Red) hung down in lank strands on his forehead. His face was thin and pale, cheeks slightly sunken in. He indicated a chair, and practically in the same movement, scratched the tip of his long, sharply pointed nose.

'Forgive me for asking all these questions,' said the girl, taking the chair he had indicated. 'But I wanted to make sure I was really talking to Red Benton. You don't look very much like a detective, Mister Benton, you must admit.'

'If you want somebody who looks like a detective,' said Red, 'you'd better get in touch with Hollywood.'

'Oh, no. I want you, Mister Benton. I've heard so much about you that I am sure you can do as I wish better than anyone else.'

Red gave a deprecating cough. 'I'm listening,' he told her. 'What exactly did you want me to do?'

'I wish to commission you to trace the man who murdered my father.'

'How about Scotland Yard? That's their job.'

'They'll never find him, I know they won't. Why, they actually had him in their hands once and allowed him to escape.'

'Suppose you begin at the beginning,' Red suggested. 'Then we'll maybe get somewhere.'

'Well first of all, I'm Mavis Pelham-Davis. As you probably read in the papers, my father was stabbed to death about a month ago. It all came out at the trial, so there is no reason why I shouldn't tell you that Father had got in the hands of a blackmailer, and for some years before his murder had been paying heavily so that the man would not bring to light certain information he possessed about an intrigue Father had had with a chorus girl in his younger days.

'The night of the murder, Father took me into his confidence and told me he was going to see this man, Gillam Waring, at his flat, and that he was going to demand — and if necessary, fight — to regain possession of the letters he had once written to this girl. The following day his body was found lying beside the railings in Berkeley Square, hardly a stone's throw from Waring's flat. Waring, of course, was unaware that Father had told anyone where he was going, and consequently never expected the deed to be traced to him. But I knew, and I communicated with the police, who picked up Waring and a great deal of evidence, including the bread knife with which Waring killed him.

'Waring stood trial and was convicted of murder in the first degree. He pleaded that Father had tried to kill him and that he had only defended himself; but the fact that no weapon was found on Father's body or in Waring's flat, and the fact that Waring was a well-known criminal character, caused the jury to bring in a charge of wilful murder. And then, while they were taking him to another prison to await execution, he knocked his guard unconscious — they were alone in the carriage — filed through the handcuff chain, and jumped from the speeding train. He has never been caught since, Mister Benton, and that was over a week ago.'

Red leaned back. 'I remember the case now,' he said. 'Didn't the papers say he was believed to have been seen in Colmouth?'

'They did, but although the police have made a wide search there, they haven't been able to pick him up.'

'And you believe I will succeed where they have failed?'

The girl nodded. 'I have read about some of the cases you have solved when the police have been baffled,' she said. 'And I would like to think that you were after this man . . . '

Red thumbed a bell push on his desk and Happy materialized in the doorway. 'Yeah, Borss?' he said enquiringly.

'Happy, did you book those train tickets for Scotland?'

'Not yet, Borss, but I'll gettem right now . . .'

'Skip it! Book two tickets for Colmouth instead — we've got a new case.'

A look of dismay crept over Happy's homely countenance. 'But Chief, you says we was goin' to Scotlan' to fish — we ain't had a vacation in two years!'

'I said Colmouth. That's a holiday place and we can mix business with pleasure. No go and book them.'

A look of infinite unhappiness crossed over Mr. Harringay's mobile face. He was not over-fond of fishing, but he had been given to understand that Scotland was where they made Scotch whisky, and one of Happy's chief obsessions was the imbibing of whisky. However, he knew better than to argue with his employer, and he nodded and withdrew.

The girl stood up. 'Thank you, Mister Benton.' She smiled. 'I feel much happier now that you are on the case.'

'It's all right, lady,' Red told her. 'Just set your mind at rest.'

'About a retainer,' she continued, fumbling in her bag. 'Will a hundred pounds be sufficient? It's all I brought.'

Red took the notes she extended and jammed them into a drawer of his desk. He hauled his feet to the floor and rose slowly.

'That'll do to be going on with,' he agreed. 'My charges for this sort of thing come pretty high, you know.'

'That doesn't matter at all. Please just send in your bill when you wish, and I will not argue about your fee.' Reaching into her bag, she brought out a printed card. She extended her hand towards him, and Red took it and glanced at the address on it. Park Lane!

'I'll send you a receipt,' he said, putting the card in a tray, 'and a schedule of my charges.'

The girl extended her hand. 'Thank you again, Mister Benton. I can't tell you how relieved I feel.'

'It's OK,' replied Red, seeing her to the door. 'So long. I'll let you have a report in due course.'

The door closed behind her.

2

Red Benton had come to England from his home town of Missoula in the state of Montana, USA. Here, amid the town's small population of 12,000 odd souls, he had created quite a reputation for himself. His methods were not all that the law could have desired, and in less than three years the powers-that-be had seen fit to suspend his license as a private detective.

Red had then made the trip to England, where he was once more free to pursue his chosen career without the necessity of being hampered by the need for a detective's license. In three years he had created a considerable reputation for himself in the old country. Starting from a shabby little office in the Tarn buildings, he had progressed in easy stages to the luxury of a modernistic office in the heart of London. His only assistant was Mister Happy Harringay, who had left America with Red, but for different reasons.

Mister Harringay's reasons were in the shape of a dead body which he was responsible for, and which he had grave doubts about the matter of explaining away. For some obscure reason the New York police never seemed to believe Mister Harringay's stories . . . and although the dead man was himself a murderer, and had at the time of his demise been endeavoring to tickle Mister Harringay's spinal column with some revolver bullets, Mister Harringay realized that he had outstayed his welcome in the great city of New York, and had deemed it expedient to seek fresh fields and pastures new . . . not that he himself would have put it quite that way.

A chance meeting with Red Benton on the beat, and the exchange of reminiscences over the poker table, had resulted in Happy accepting a position within the law, as Red's junior partner. Although not very strong in brain, Mister Harringay was blessed with more than his fair share of brawn; and, into the bargain, was a very handy gentleman with a revolver — or as he termed it, a 'betsy'. They had faced many dangers together since their meeting, and had naturally developed a certain hidden attachment to one another; but apart from this they had little in common.

So when Red Benton paused to study a flamboyant poster outside the station, after a very tiring journey down to Colmouth in the county of Kent; and when he remarked that he 'must see that' and instructed Happy to obtain two tickets for the opening of the Granada Palace Concert Hall, Happy let out a startled yelp.

'But, Borss! That's a performance strictly for the long underwear department — you knows I hates highbrow stuff, Borss! Jeez! Ya couldn't expec' me to latch on to that, could youse?'

Mister Harringay was right when he said that the poster applied only to the — as he termed it — 'long underwear department.' Mister Harringay was a lover of Duke Ellington and Tommy Dorsey and Harry James. He liked his music 'hot,' and the advertisement on the poster filled him with ominous forebodings.

It was a brilliant poster, one calculated to catch the eye. It stated that after being closed for twenty years, the Granada Palace Concert Hall would open on the following Monday evening with a performance of a new concerto by a new composer. The title of the concerto was 'Concerto for Fear', and, the bill added, it had been composed by a certain Peter Innis.

It was this fact that had caught the eye of Red Benton. The knowledge that the orchestra would be under the baton of Sergi Lestivoff worried him not at all, but Peter Innis he knew and liked. He had once been responsible for extracting Peter from a sticky jam. A famous violinist had lost his Stradivarius while playing at the Albert Hall. He had accused Innis, who was attached to the orchestra, of taking it from his room. Red had been called in by Innis, and had found that the violinist had hidden away his own violin in order to claim the insurance money on the same. Red had promptly exposed the man and cleared Innis, and a firm friendship with the young pianist had been the result.

Therefore, whatever Mister Harringay liked or did not like, it was only natural that Red should feel pleased that Peter had finally composed an important piece, and that he should experience a natural desire to be there on the first night. So it was that a lugubrious Mister Harringay found himself purchasing two tickets for the performance of a new concerto.

'Borss,' said Happy, handing the tickets to Red, 'why you wanta lug me into this thing? Why not let me go around the saloons here, while youse take in the show, huh?'

'Because I have no desire to have to haul you out of the police station and carry your whisky-logged carcass home in the small hours of the morning. No, don't object, Happy. It's happened before, and it'll happen again — but not at the moment. You are going to the concerto, and, like it or not, you are going to applaud until your fingernails drop off. Or else . . . ' concluded Red darkly.

And Happy had to be content. So that, the very evening of their arrival, found Red and Happy — wriggling and perspiring in the clutches of a stiff collar — making their way to the Granada Palace.

Most of Colmouth's population appeared to be making their way in the same direction. Colmouth was a refined town, patronized by London's smarter set, and it seemed that the concerto was due to go down with a bang, from first to last.

Having stowed Happy safely in his seat, Red made his way to the stage door and asked for Mister Innis. Peter Innis arrived in no time, looking a little flushed and excited. He was tall and well-built and had the typically healthy-looking face of a man who spends the best part of his life out of doors. He was hardly representative of the musician. When he saw Red, his eyes lit up, and he bounded forward and pumped his friend's hand vigorously.

'Red, you old ass,' he bawled heartily. 'What a slice of luck seeing you!'

'How're things with you, Pete?' Red asked him.

'Couldn't be better. I suppose you've seen the bills?'

'About the concerto? Sure. I don't

suppose I am the first to congratulate you, but I do. I'm darn glad you made it at last, you old faker.'

'It was the most unexpected piece of luck — I'd written the blessed thing, then I left it kicking around for a time. I don't know if I told you, but I'm engaged to rather a nice girl — ' Peter blushed furiously. 'Alice Graham, the daughter of Sir Alexander Graham.'

'The well-known symphonic conductor?'

'The same. Well, Alice happened to get hold of this thing I'd written, and she knew the owners of the Granada were contemplating opening up again. And she, being a friend of the chairman's, took my piece along. You can imagine my surprise when they agreed to make it the main item on the programme, old man.'

'I hope, for your sake, it's a big hit,' said Red sincerely.

Peter clenched his fists. 'It's got to be, Red! You see, if it is, arrangements will be made to have it played at the Albert Hall — no, it isn't the money or the glory I'm thinking of, Red. It's Alice's father. He thinks I'm a no-good young ass — you

17

know what these old martinets are — and until I've done something worthwhile, he won't give his consent to our marriage. But when this is played at the Albert Hall, he can't refuse very well, can he? So you see, it just *has* to be a hit!'

Red slapped his back encouragingly. 'I'm sure it will be, Pete. I guess you'll be at the piano yourself?'

'No, that's the rotten part of it all. I twisted my wrist the other week, and I can't manage it. But we've got a fine pianist, and I know he'll do justice to it. And by the time they're ready for it in London, I'll be all right again.'

They talked for some time longer, then Red took his leave and returned to the front of the house. Mister Harringay was shuffling his feet uncomfortably and running a sticky finger round the inside of his collar. 'When do they finish, Borss?' he begged.

'Finish? You piecan, they haven't started yet!'

'They ain't?' yelped Happy. 'But Borss, they been tweeting their fiddles for the last half hour!'

'You nut,' grinned Red. 'They're only tuning up!'

Happy emitted a subdued groan. More of the orchestra took their positions at the stand, the lights went dimmer, and there was a round of applause as the conductor took the stand. He raised his arm . . .

3

Red Benton was by no means a fan of highbrow music, but he had to admit that Peter Innis had written an excellent piece in his 'Concerto for Fear'. The allegro was stirring, inducing strange thoughts in the minds of the listeners. The great concert hall was dead quiet, hardly a cough disturbing the spell of the music. Even Happy appeared to be enjoying it more than he would have thought possible.

Then came the piano solo. With lightning-like rapidity the pianist's hands shot up and down the keyboard, blending note into note in a melody of unearthly harmony. The solo concluded on a clashing discord, and the orchestra prepared to accompany again . . .

But before they could commence, the pianist, a look of horror on his face, half rose from his stool, clutched at his breast, and slumped to the platform floor!

For almost thirty seconds no one moved or spoke. Then a cry of horror went up from the audience and they came to their feet simultaneously.

The conductor ran to the side of the recumbent pianist, knelt and swiftly examined him. Then he gestured to the two nearest members of the orchestra. With looks of incredibility they hurried forward, and the inert pianist was hastily carried from the stage.

The conductor reappeared, white in the face. He raised a hand to silence the noisy cries of consternation and enquiry. 'Ladies and gentlemen,' he called. 'Our pianist has been taken — ill. If there is a doctor here we should be glad of his services.'

A short tubby man near Red and Happy stood up and began to push towards the platform.

'Thank you,' said the conductor. 'Will you come through the pass door, sir?' The doctor nodded and made for the pass door at the side of the auditorium. Red Benton stood up.

'Stick here, Happy. I'm going back

stage — seems to be some funny business about this.' He followed the tubby doctor and vanished through the door after him.

In the wings there was an uproar. Stretched out on the floorboards was the pianist. On his white shirt front in the region of the heart, an ugly red stain was beginning to spread. His face was waxen and he lay perfectly still and quiet. The doctor bent over him, made a rapid examination.

'What — what is it, doctor?' asked Peter Innis, who stood near, running his hands through his hair distractedly.

'He's quite dead,' the tubby man replied. 'Shot right through the heart I should say — death almost instantaneous.'

'My God!' Peter Innis whispered. 'The poor devil!' He turned away and for the first time saw Red. 'Red! Glad you're here — you saw?'

Red nodded. 'Hadn't you better send for the police?' he told him. 'And post attendants to see that no one leaves the place until they arrive.'

'Of course . . . I'll phone now,' replied

22

Peter, dashing towards a small office near the stage.

Red crossed and stood above the dead man. From the front of the house could be heard a babble of voices and questions.

The dead man was about thirty-five. He was dark and clean-shaven and had obviously had a good-humored, round face in life. But at the moment it was contorted with shock.

Red turned to the jittery conductor. 'Who was he?' he demanded.

'Charles Nichols,' the conductor said dazedly. 'He often plays with us when we need a substitute pianist.'

'Know if he had any enemies?'

'I'm afraid not — he always seemed a likeable sort of chap though, and I never heard of him having any.'

'Did you hear the shot?' queried Red.

'No, I heard nothing — knew nothing until I saw him fall.'

'Any of you fellows hear the shot?' Red turned to the rest of the orchestra, who had gathered round in a bunch. They shook their heads.

'Nor did I,' Red mused. 'Silencer, obviously.' He looked at the dead man again. 'Was he married?'

'He was — ' said the conductor. 'I believe his wife died last year, leaving him with an eight-year-old girl — God knows how anyone will be able to break the news to the poor child.'

Red shook his head slowly. 'It's a tough world,' he agreed. He stooped and examined the wound more closely. 'He was sitting on the right-hand side of the stage as the audience would see him,' he said thoughtfully, 'with his left side facing the audience. The bullet seems to have gone in at an angle, so that anyone on the right-hand side of the auditorium might have fired the shot — or, it could have been fired from the side of the platform at a pinch . . . ' He turned to the doctor. 'Would you say the shot had been fired close to, or from a distance?'

The doctor shook his head. 'That would be hard to say — you'd need a ballistics expert to even give you an idea.'

Peter Innis returned from the phone. 'This is awful,' he said worriedly. 'The police will be here in a few minutes — I've instructed the attendants to hold the audience, but it seems that some of them have already gone home.'

'Brace up, Pete. It isn't your fault if somebody wanted to bump the man off. They'd probably have done it anyway.'

A tall, distinguished, grey-haired man pushed through the circle.

'Mister Hallam!' exclaimed Peter. 'Did you see what happened?'

Hallam nodded. 'I was in front — a terrible thing to happen on the first night. Why, it could mean that we won't be able to keep the place open after all . . . '

'And that,' said Red coldly, 'would be terrible, eh?'

'It certainly would,' snapped Hallam. 'After all these years of being closed down, we thought that the Granada would at last be able to hold its own and make back a little of the money we've lost on it . . . '

'Mister Hallam is the principal director,' explained Peter.

'Really,' drawled Red, unimpressed. 'There's a dead man on the floor, and I don't think it matters a great deal whether Mister Hallam makes money or not at the moment.' He turned his back on the director, who had gone red in the face, and proceeded to ignore him completely. Followed by Peter Innis, Red walked onto the platform and over to the piano. Paying no attention to the excited audience, he sat down on the stool and gazed about. Suddenly his gaze became fixed. He leaned forward and stared at the piano lid, which was raised.

Halfway up the raised keyboard lid, on the end nearest the audience, was a small hole in the wood!

Red whistled and lowered the lid. He noted a second hole in the thin panel on which the back of the lid rested. He stood up and peered inside the piano, leaning far over the open top. Then he motioned to Peter to join him. 'There's your killer,' he said shortly, pointing to a neat black thirty-two automatic strapped under a side beam inside the grand, the muzzle pointing in a direct line with the piano stool.

Peter looked incredulously at the

detective. 'That must be it,' he gasped. 'But how the devil was it fired while the concerto was being played?'

Red inserted his hand in the piano and fumbled about. 'There's a thin wire,' he explained. 'It's fastened onto one of the piano key hammers.' He made a closer examination.

'How many times did he play this note?' Red demanded, touching bottom G. Peter thought a moment.

'Only once,' he said.

'Then that's it,' Red told him. 'The instant he played that note the firing mechanism operated and the deed was done!'

4

Inspector Lakeman of the Colmouth limbs of the law was a fat, red-visaged man with a perpetual grudge against life. That grudge was in operation when he arrived at the Granada with two constables and the divisional surgeon, shortly after the murder had been committed.

He was annoyed, extremely annoyed. Only the previous day his wife had purchased two tickets for the concerto, and Lakeman had wanted very much to attend the opening. But the pressure of work had made his presence at the station indispensable, and through that fact he had missed a murder which might have happened under his very nose!

He burst in like a stout whirlwind, and within two minutes — while the surgeon conducted his examination — he had everyone on the platform flustered and flummoxed with questions.

'You kept the audience here?' he demanded.

'Er — yes,' replied Peter. 'But . . . '

'Dawson, Hoskins!' bawled the Inspector to his subordinates. 'Take up positions at the main doors and have the audience file out past you — give them a quick examination for concealed weapons.'

'I don't think that will be needed,' put in Red, who was aware that Mister Harringay 'toted a betsy.'

Lakeman whirled on him. 'And who the devil are you to say what's needed and what's not?' he roared. 'The murderer must be somewhere in this building, and I'll have him, or go back to pounding the beat!'

'Then you'd better get your boots soled and heeled,' Red suggested. 'Because I doubt very much whether you'll find the murderer in the audience.'

'Who are you?' howled the inspector.

Peter Innis coughed tactfully. 'This is Mister Benton,' he said. 'Red Benton, the well-known detective, Inspector.'

The inspector peered closely at Red. He frowned. 'Oh, so you're Red Benton, are you?' he grunted. 'Well Mister Benton, I've heard all about you and I'm not sure I like what I've heard. Anyway,

I'm quite capable of handling this case without your assistance. I'm not a member of the London police force,' he added sarcastically.

Red smiled. 'I only thought I'd save you a bit of trouble, Inspector,' he said. 'But never mind, carry on.'

The two constables went about their duties and the inspector started firing questions at all and sundry. When he had finished he was no nearer a solution, and he turned to Red thoughtfully, scratching his head. 'What did you mean, Benton, by saying it was no use searching the audience?' he barked.

Red shook his head. 'It doesn't matter, Inspector.' He smiled.

'But it does matter,' snorted Lakeman. 'I want to know . . . ' He broke off as one of the constables returned, dragging a very reluctant Mister Harringay by the arm.

'I found this man carrying a revolver, sir,' said the PC, glowing with honest pride.

'Hah!' snorted Lakeman. 'Good work, Dawson!'

'Hello, Borss,' said Mister Harringay, nodding to Red.

'Hello Happy,' Red returned.

'What's all this?' barked Lakeman. 'You two know each other?'

'My assistant,' explained Red.

'So . . . ' said the inspector, like the villain in an old-time melodrama. 'Carrying a revolver, was he? Where is it?'

'He won't give it to me,' said the constable with an injured expression.

'Give the inspector your revolver, Happy,' Red ordered.

'But Borss, I don't like being wit'out my betsy,' pleaded Happy mournfully.

'He'll give it back,' Red told him.

Dolefully, Mister Harringay handed over his beloved betsy. The inspector's eyes gleamed.

'So you two have been up to something, eh? You'll find it hard to explain this away!'

'Not at all — Happy has a license. And in any case, I think you'll find that the gun is still fully loaded — not a single shot fired. Is there, Happy?'

'That's right, all right, Borss.' Happy said, nodding.

'Huh!' grunted Lakeman, unimpressed.

'He could have loaded it again after the murder.'

'Aren't you making a serious accusation there?' said Red in a steely tone.

The inspector realized he was going ahead too fast. 'Anyway,' he snapped, 'I'm holding him on suspicion.'

'I don't think so,' Red told him. 'You see, Happy's gun is a forty-five — whereas the killing was done by a thirty-two.'

The inspector looked blank. Then he jumped and fixed Red with a triumphant eye. 'You've given yourself away, Benton! How'd you know it was a thirty-two revolver when we haven't got the bullet yet?'

Red sighed wearily and lit a cigarette. 'Come with me,' he said. 'If you'd listened at first when I tried to tell you, you'd have saved all this trouble.' He took the distrustful inspector over and pointed out the gun inside the piano. The inspector returned a wiser and more thoughtful man.

'You can let that man go,' he rapped to the constable.

'Let — let him g-go, sir?' stuttered that worthy.

'Yes man!' bawled the inspector. 'Are you deaf?'

The constable released Happy as if he had been a handful of molten lead.

'And go and tell Hoskins he needn't search any longer.'

'He — he needn't?' stammered Dawson.

The inspector fixed him with an awful frown, and Dawson flew.

'Now,' said Lakeman in a subdued tone. 'Will everyone who has had access to this piano within the last week, line up here.'

The entire orchestra, Peter Innis, and the caretaker of the building lined up.

'How about you?' barked the inspector, turning to Hallam.

'I haven't . . . ' began Hallam.

'Yes, you have,' said Peter. 'Don't you remember? You came to rehearsals last week.'

'Of — of course. Sorry, Inspector . . . ' Hallam joined the line and the inspector regarded them fiercely.

'Anyone know anything about this gun in this piano?' he barked.

Peter Innis stepped forward.

33

'Did you know the gun was here?' barked Lakeman.

'Yes, Inspector. Mister Benton showed it to me just before you came.'

The Inspector's eyes almost popped out. 'I meant before the murder!' he roared.

'Sorry,' said Peter, stepping back.

'You should be! Downright stupid to answer the question at all,' yapped the inspector.

'You were rather stupid to ask it,' observed Red. 'It isn't likely that anyone would answer a question like that — or were you hoping for a miracle?'

The inspector tore his scanty locks and clutched his brow. 'Will you keep out of this,' he yelped. 'I'm trying to do my job, aren't I?'

'Trying is right,' agreed Red.

The suspects watched Lakeman with considerable awe. He seemed to be in imminent danger of exploding. His features had gone a brilliant red, and his collar appeared to be choking him. 'Perhaps you'd care to take over, Mister Benton,' he snarled in a voice of sarcastic politeness.

'I'd be pleased.' Red grinned, and pushing the man aside he confronted the suspects.

The inspector was flabbergasted. He stood with his mouth opening and shutting feebly, unable to recover himself.

'Mister Hallam,' said Red. 'Do you understand music?'

'Er — yes, a little,' agreed Hallam.

'Thank you! Of course, all you gentlemen of the orchestra do, don't you?'

'I can answer for that,' smiled the conductor. 'If they didn't, they would hardly be here.'

Lakeman pushed forward again. 'What the devil's understanding music got to do with it?' he almost shrieked.

'Quiet please,' said Red. He turned to the caretaker — a shriveled, dark-faced man. 'Do you?'

The caretaker glanced round. The conductor spoke for him. 'Yes, Lipton understands music,' he said. 'Perhaps better than any of us. He used to be a famous pianist himself in his day — until he lost three fingers off his right hand.'

'That's right,' said Hallam. 'He was

involved in an accident in which he lost his fingers — that made it impossible for him to play again, and we gave him the job here as caretaker, since he often used to play here in the old days before the place closed down.'

'You still understand music, Lipton?' asked Red.

'Yes sir,' mumbled the old caretaker.

'Thank you. So, any of you gentlemen would have understood enough about the score of Innis's concerto to have known that bottom G was played only once during the performance?'

They nodded.

'You see, Inspector, it seems that the man who planned the murder wanted it to happen at the psychological moment — at the end of the piano solo. It would be necessary for him to have had a knowledge of music to have arranged that — and also to have had access to the score of 'Concerto for Fear'. Which of you could have read the score?'

'Any of us,' said the conductor. 'It was lying on the piano for a week during rehearsals.'

'Did any of you know the dead man particularly well?'

Nobody answered.

'Thank you,' said Red. He gestured to the inspector. 'You can carry on now, Inspector.'

'Have you quite finished?' demanded Lakeman in a sulfurous voice.

'Quite.'

'And may I ask what you have found out — if anything?'

'I prefer to retain that information,' said Red pleasantly. He motioned to Mister Harringay, who was going to sleep against the piano. 'Come, Happy — let us leave the inspector to his masterly examination!'

They strolled out of the theater, leaving the inspector brimming with impotent fury.

5

Red Benton yawned luxuriously, stretched, slid out of bed and into his slippers and dressing gown and headed for the bathroom. The Pavilion Hotel at Colmouth was an excellent hotel. The food was good, the accommodation was superb, and the chambermaids were exceedingly attractive. Red was finding his stay there quite enjoyable. And so, evidently, was Happy Harringay; for as Red passed, from that gentleman's door issued the sound of prodigious snoring.

Red smiled, took a quick bath, dressed, and went down to breakfast, leaving the sleeping beauty to it.

He was just finishing the toast and marmalade in the dining room, when a fat figure appeared in the doorway and blinked inquisitively round. It was Inspector Lakeman in the flesh — and plenty of it. Spotting Red, he crossed the room and sank into a vacant chair opposite. He had obviously got over his tantrums of the previous night, for his features were quite humble. He coughed deprecatingly and tapped the cloth.

'Morning, Inspector,' volunteered Red, lighting a cigarette. 'Have one?' He extended his case.

'No thanks,' said Lakeman. 'Don't smoke. Wife won't . . . er — I mean I don't believe in it.'

Red smiled and waited. The inspector coughed again. He seemed to be having considerable trouble coming to the point.

'Look here, Benton, I admit I was a bit rattled last night,' he began. 'But . . . '

'That's all right,' Red told him. 'Afraid I got your goat a bit. Faults on both sides. Forgive and forget, shall we?'

The inspector nodded. 'This case has got me stumped,' he said sadly. 'I can't make head or tail of it — almost anybody might have done it.'

'No motive?'

'None at all. Lipton wasn't very well known to anyone, it seems.'

'No prints on the gun?'

'No, not one. That's the funny thing

— we've traced the man the gun was issued to . . . '

'That'll be helpful, won't it? Who was it?'

'That's the awkward part — that's why I can't understand it at all. You see, it was issued to Gillam Waring.'

Red sat bolt upright. 'Waring? The blackmailer who was convicted of murder and escaped?'

The inspector nodded.

'That's very, very interesting,' mused Red.

'Not to me it isn't,' said Lakeman gloomily. 'Where the hell does Waring come into it? Did he do the murder? If so, why? These are things which need answering — and I'm supposed to answer them. If I don't get somewhere soon they'll call the Yard in, and spoil the only chance I've ever had to make a name for myself!'

'Skip the motive for a moment,' Red said thoughtfully, 'and let's weigh things up. Doesn't it strike you as funny that anyone who had a feud with Lipton should choose such a dramatic means of murdering him? I mean, just at that point in the concerto. Don't you think they could have found a quieter and less conspicuous method of eliminating him?'

'It does seem a bit funny,' agreed Lakeman reflectively. 'But why did they kill him, if they hadn't a reason for wishing to do so?'

'Perhaps they'd have killed anyone who'd sat at that piano. Suppose there'd been a substitute playing at the last minute — they couldn't have stopped him being shot, could they? Add to that the fact that the bullet needn't necessarily have killed the man — there was no one to sight it on his heart — it was more bad luck than anything that he got it in a fatal spot.'

'But if they hadn't anything against Lipton, why kill him at all?'

'Suppose they wanted to ruin the concerto?'

'But why?'

'Well, they could have it in for Innis — or, possibly, they don't want the Granada to open up again . . . '

'But that's only guesswork!'

Red nodded. 'I know, but we have to explore the possibilities. Now doesn't it strike you as peculiar that Waring's gun was the one to do the deed — and that Waring himself was reported as having been seen in Colmouth only last week?'

'It does. We've scoured the town from end to end, but we can't find any trace of him. I think the man who made the report must have been mistaken . . . '

'But in the light of finding Waring's gun here — do you still think he was mistaken?'

'I'm beginning to think not.'

'Let's look at another angle. During the last few years I have noticed that quite a number of well-known criminals who have been on the run, have been seen in Colmouth. They've never been picked up, however, and shortly afterwards they've been spotted on the Continent. What does this signify?'

Lakeman shook his head helplessly.

'Think it over, Inspector. I haven't quite worked it all out myself yet, but I'll see that you're in at the kill — if there is any kill!'

The inspector nodded and took his leave shortly afterwards. Red completed his breakfast, washed it down with strong coffee, lit another cigarette and left the hotel. He wandered down to the Granada Palace Concert Hall, but instead of going in through the stage door he walked to the rear of the building.

The Granada Palace was built on the extreme edge of a rocky headland, the back overlooking the sea. A set of roughly cut steps, hacked in the rock, led up to a small door at the rear of the Granada and Red studied these with interest for some time. Then he made his way to the stage door.

He discovered Peter Innis on the stage, gazing ruefully at the piano.

'Hello, Red,' Peter exclaimed. 'Come down to have a look round?'

Red shook his head. 'Not at the piano,' he said. 'I was wondering if you have any cellars under this place?'

Peter knitted his brows. 'Blowed if I know — we can soon find out though.'

'It's all right,' Red told him. 'I'll take a stroll round myself if you don't mind.' He crossed to the back of the platform, where on the right-hand side a flight of steps led downwards. At the bottom was a long red-and-cream-painted passage with doors off it. These, apparently, were dressing rooms.

Red walked right past them and continued on down the passage. Hardly visible in the gloom down there was a dark opening. Red pulled a pen-torch from his pocket and shone it down the opening. There were steps running down. He descended cautiously.

He was in a long, low cellar. At regular intervals, wooden beams ran upwards to support the platform above. Littered all over the place were pieces of scenery, old rostrums, baskets, props, and all the odds and ends which go to make up the rubbish department of the average theatre.

Red shone his torch all about, then began to examine the scenery which was resting against the walls.

There was a sudden burst of melody from the platform over his head, and he heard the opening bars of the 'Concerto for Fear' being played. He went on with his search, subconsciously listening to the melody as he did so.

The pianist came to the end of the solo piece, finishing with the weird discord. Then without warning, the playing stopped, and there was a heavy thud on the floor above Red.

He paused, stiffened, and listened. For some seconds all was silent. Then hurried feet ran across the stage. A voice was audible, calling, 'Red — Red! Where are you?'

Red raced across the cellar and up the stairs. Peter met him in the passage, a strained expression on his suntanned face.

'What's happened?' demanded Red.

'The new pianist — the one who was going to play tonight — he just arrived from London, and was trying the concerto over.'

'I heard him,' Red admitted. 'But what happened? He stopped.'

'He's dead,' panted Peter weakly. 'Just got off the stool and flopped right out!'

6

'It's the limit,' said Inspector Lakeman wearily. 'First a man gets shot, now a man gets poisoned! Poisoned! By the same piano! How did you say it was done, Benton?'

Red nodded towards the piano. 'If you look on that bottom G again,' he said, 'you'll see that a hole has been drilled in it — a small hole. A thin needle has been inserted in the hole and tipped with deadly poison.'

'My God,' moaned Lakeman. 'How much longer are these murders going to go on? Who's behind it all? This chap wasn't known to anybody down here at all. What's at the back of this game? And who?'

Peter Innis stood with clenched fists. His face was white and troubled, and Red knew he was hard hit. Apart from the tragedy of the two deaths, the concerto meant a lot to Innis. It meant he would prove himself to the father of the girl he loved, and that he would achieve a certain status in the musical world once it had been played at the Albert Hall. But as yet the concerto hadn't been played half through.

'We can't get another pianist in time,' said Peter slowly. 'I expect this means we'll have to close down.'

'And if this effort fails it means the Granada will have to close also,' remarked Hallam, who had been sent for.

The conductor stepped forward. 'We can't let ourselves be beaten like this,' he said quietly. 'If Mister Innis will lead the orchestra tonight, I will volunteer to play the piano.'

'But it isn't safe!' exclaimed Hallam. 'It's silly to put yourself in danger, man!'

Sergi Lestivoff smiled. 'If the piano is thoroughly examined before I begin to play, I see no reason why there should be any danger,' he said.

Peter Innis grasped his hand. 'Thanks, Mister Lestivoff,' he said. 'It means a lot to me to have this concerto played right through.'

'Wait a minute,' barked Lakeman.

'Don't I have anything to say about this?'

'Inspector,' said Red, 'you do. But you can't close the place down — that isn't within your province — and if you do you will probably never catch the murderer.'

Lakeman nodded. 'I suppose you're right — but if anyone else gets killed there'll be a riot! How did the murderer manage to put the needle there in the first place?'

'Most likely in the night,' Red suggested. 'I take it you didn't leave a guard, did you? No, of course you didn't. You had no way of knowing there would be a second murder. Well, if all goes well this evening, Inspector, I would suggest that you leave a man to watch the place tonight.'

'I will,' barked the inspector grimly. 'I certainly will!'

With the aid of a pair of pliers loaned by the caretaker, the poisoned needle was extracted by Lakeman and placed in an envelope. The ambulance arrived, and the body was carried out.

'Forget it all for a while,' said Red to the puzzled inspector. 'Let's go along the front and have coffee somewhere.'

The inspector nodded agreement and so did Peter Innis. But Lestivoff shook his head. 'I think I'll stay here and run over the concerto.' He smiled. 'I want to have it perfect for tonight.'

'If you're going to play that damned concerto,' snapped Lakeman, 'I'd better tell the ambulance boys to wait a while so they can pick up another body!'

The conductor smiled and began to thoroughly examine the death-dealing piano. At last he sat down before the keyboard. 'There can't possibly be anything wrong with it now,' he said.

'Just the same,' argued Lakeman, 'I'll wait and see you play it through once . . . '

$$\star \quad \star \quad \star$$

The conductor started to play. He had a wonderful touch and even Lakeman lost himself in the magic of the 'Concerto for Fear'. As he came to the fatal bottom G, the onlookers tensed; then, with a firm finger, he drove the note down, and carried on.

'Whew!' gasped Lakeman, breathing

again. 'Thank the Lord it didn't kill that time — I would have heard about it if it had!'

'All right, inspector, you can go now,' smiled Lestivoff.

'Stay here for a time,' Lakeman told him. 'As I pass the station I'll send a constable along, and when you're through practicing he can take over and keep an eye on the piano until tonight. That way we'll be sure it isn't tampered with!'

The conductor smiled and went on playing. They could hear him going strong as they passed outside.

Here the caretaker broke off and started to walk in the other direction which led to his home. The three men — Red, Peter and the inspector — continued on down the front for a time until they reached the station. Here Lakeman slipped inside, but returned shortly with Constable Dawson by his side, wearing an eager-to-please look.

'Dawson'll watch the grand,' explained Lakeman. He turned to the constable. 'Go along to the Granada — you'll find the conductor there playing the piano.

When he's finished, take over, and don't leave the side of that piano until the concert starts tonight. You understand?'

Dawson looked anxious. He shuffled his feet.

'Well, man? What the devil's wrong with you?' stormed Lakeman irritably.

Dawson coughed apologetically. 'Begging your pardon, 'spector,' he mumbled. 'But I 'aven't 'ad me dinner yet . . . '

Lakeman appeared to be on the verge of an apoplectic stroke. '*Dinner!*' he roared. 'Damnit, man, what does your dinner matter? Do as I tell you!'

The abashed constable gulped, flushed, and hurried away.

'Dinner!' hissed Lakeman, boiling with fury. 'What have I done to be saddled with men who would be more at home on the inside of a lunatic asylum? Dinner!'

They proceeded towards a café, Lakeman erupting at various intervals.

After coffee, Red left the other two and returned to his hotel. In the bar he found Happy Harringay putting himself on the right side of some Scotch. Stretched along the bar in front of his assistant were a dozen glasses. They had obviously been full, but were now empty. Happy was wearing a slightly dazed look, and the barman a bewildered expression.

Red grabbed the stumpy American's shoulder and jerked. 'You mutt-head!' he rapped. 'What use are you to me, sodden with booze?'

'It's OK, Borss,' hiccupped Happy. 'I ain't drunk!'

Red led him over to a small table. 'Listen,' he said. 'I want you to do something. If you're sober enough . . . '

'Sure, Borss — whaddya wan' doin'?' In spite of the whisky he had taken, Happy was still reasonably sober.

'Take my skeleton keys,' Red told him. 'And make your way to a little door at the back of the Granada Palace. Open it, go in, and search the cellar. Be quiet and keep your eyes peeled. If you see anything suspicious, phone me at once.'

'Huh?'

'I said phone me.'

'Where'll you be?'

'I have to get back to London — I'm testifying in the Lane case today. But I'll be back tonight for sure. And by the way — if you can't find anything strange in the cellars, lie low in there behind some scenery and watch for a while. If I don't hear from you before I get back I'll meet you at seven o'clock. Have you got it right?'

'Sure, Borss,' Happy said. He paused uncertainly. 'Borss, it's liable to be dry work waitin' in a cellar — is it okay for me to take a bottle o' hooch down with me?'

'It is not,' barked Red. 'If I think you've been at the bottle when I get back, I'll knock you silly! Now, on your way!'

With a glum expression, Mister Harringay left the hotel.

Red himself caught the first London train and arrived at the courtrooms just in time to be called to the stand. It did not take the jury long to reach a verdict, and he was free again sooner than he had expected. He took a cab to his office to see if there was any correspondence for him before returning to Colmouth. While he was there the telephone rang. He recognized the voice as that of Mavis Pelham-Davis.

'Oh, Mister Benton,' she cooed. 'I've been ringing you up all day — I noticed you were due to testify in the Lane case, and I guessed you'd be back in London today, so I thought I'd try to get in touch with you. Have you found anything out?'

'Nothing of much importance, Miss Davis,' Red replied. 'But I've got one or two good ideas — in fact, my assistant is putting one of them into operation right now.'

'That's wonderful. You *will* let me know if anything happens, won't you?'

'I will.'

'I've been reading about that murder at the Granada Palace,' she said. 'It must have been terribly exciting.'

'Not for the murdered man's young daughter,' snapped Red dryly.

'Oh, were you there?'

'I was. Well, good night, Miss Davis . . .'

'But Mister Benton, I hadn't finished . . .'

'I had,' snapped Red, and slammed down the phone. He detested women who gloated over murder cases.

7

Red was a little late arriving back at Colmouth. First the phone call from the Davis girl had delayed him, and then his taxi to the station had got into a traffic jam, and the driver had had hot words with one of the stalwarts of the law while Red had fumed impatiently in the rear. All of this had caused him to miss the train he had planned on catching, and when he finally tumbled out of the first-class smoker at Colmouth, a glance at his wrist watch told him it was already seven thirty.

He deliberated for a minute over whether to head straight for the Pavilion Hotel or whether to go right to the Granada. Eventually he decided on the Granada — after all, he had told Happy to meet him at the hotel at seven, and possibly Happy had already given up hopes of his arrival and had gone to the concert hall himself. In any case, he could contact his assistant after the show.

He particularly wanted to be at the Granada for the concerto. There was that in his mind which told him that tonight was going to be no exception — that something else was due to happen, as it had on the preceding evening.

He turned out of the station, down Alby Street, and onto the Promenade. It was swell out there, with the sun dipping down behind the horizon and a light breeze sweeping in from the sea and stroking the burning sand, fluttering the massive ferns which were planted in the small square gardens all along the Prom. Red filled his lungs with air, then lit a cigarette. He inhaled deeply, and for a moment stood leaning on the low sea wall, thinking that someday — when so many people weren't killing so many other people — he'd like to come to a place like this and lie on the sands and stroll in the parks, and maybe have a round or two on the golf course which fronted straight onto the beach at the lower end of the Prom.

He examined his watch again, noted the time was 7:45, and moved more rapidly towards the Granada. He went down to the stage door, nodded to the caretaker, who also acted as doorman at the back, and went on into the concert hall.

The symphony orchestra were just tuning up — Peter Innis, dressed in tails, was standing on the side of the platform looking more strained and worried than he had done so far. Red tapped him on the arm, and he jumped.

'Red! Thank God you're back.'

'Why, what's happened?'

'Nothing,' said Peter bitterly. 'Nothing at all — except that after we left Lestivoff here this morning, he vanished!'

'He what?' yelped Red.

'Vanished! When Dawson arrived he was nowhere to be found. Dawson thought he'd probably left the place, and didn't bother to tell anyone until Lakeman came to see how Dawson was getting on. When we found out we tried everywhere, searched everywhere. No good. He'd simply disappeared. Yet we left him alone in the building.'

'But there'd have been plenty of time for someone to sneak in on him and do the job, and leave again before Dawson got there.'

'But how on earth could they leave with a full-grown man — even if they knocked him unconscious?'

'If I knew that I'd probably know the answer. So now he's gone, the concerto won't go on — or will it?'

'It will.' said Peter grimly. 'One of the orchestra boys will conduct, and I myself will play the piano part — I'm afraid it won't be up to standard with this strained wrist, but I'm determined it will be played!'

'Have you thoroughly examined the piano?'

Peter nodded. 'Every square inch,' he said.

Red gripped his hand as the orchestra quietened their tuning and he prepared to go on stage. Peter smiled, a trifle somberly, and went on stage.

The concerto commenced and Red listened mechanically, but his eyes were on the alert, searching the stage and audience for anything which might spell danger.

Considering his injured wrist, Peter played the solo remarkably well, and undoubtedly the whole thing would have gone off excellently, but for the body . . .

The body happened about the usual point in the solo — just at the sounding of the final bottom G.

It came flying down from the ceiling, narrowly missing Peter at the piano, and landed with a sickening crunch of bone, right at the front of the platform.

The audience had been almost expecting something of the sort — or at least, amongst the more perverse, hoping for it. Now they came to their feet with a simultaneous yell.

'Drop the curtain!' cried Peter, taking in the situation at a glance. One of the stage hands pulled the lever that operated the heavy brocaded semi-circular front curtain, and the scene was cut off from the audience.

'Lestivoff,' said Peter, bending over the body as Red hurried forward.

Red looked at the mangled face, almost unrecognizable, then at the savagely shattered head at the back. In spite of his professional hardness he felt a little sick.

'There's a rope round his waist — looks like one of the ropes they use to raise and lower the backcloths,' whispered Peter.

Red picked up the free end of the rope, examined it, and glanced up towards the roof. 'Pretty clear what's happened,' he said. 'He's been dead for some time — probably murdered since just after we left him. He must have been murdered and hauled up and concealed in the folds of the front curtain before Dawson arrived, which shows that whoever did it knows that you aren't bothering to raise and lower that curtain. If it had been lowered and raised at the start of the performance, the body wouldn't have been concealed. So they tied a rope round his middle, hoisted him up, secured the other end of the rope at the side of the stage and, when the moment came, slashed through it with a knife! Obviously it must have been someone on the side of the stage who did the rope-cutting trick — but who?'

He glanced at the stage. There were two or three stagehands; Hallam, the director; and the caretaker. Red stood up, went over to the caretaker, and halted in front of him.

'Aren't you supposed to be on duty at the stage door?'

'Yes, sir — but I heard some excitement and came to see what was wrong.'

Red swung away back to Peter. 'Pete,' he said in a low tone, 'send for Lakeman — and keep these people talking here while I'm gone. Particularly the caretaker.'

'Why, what are you going to do?'

'Search his jacket — I see he isn't wearing it, and I conclude he must have left it in his office at the door. There might just be a missing clue in that!'

Peter nodded and crossed to the little knot of people. Red slid down the passage to the stage door and tried it.

It was locked. Red smiled grimly: the caretaker couldn't have left in such a hurry if he'd had time to lock his office.

Red felt in his pockets and cursed as he remembered giving his master keys to Happy. But there was a small window in the front of the office, at which enquiries were answered. Red peered through it and found that by straining his arm he could just reach the jacket, which was hanging on a peg behind the door. He

61

slipped it from the peg and pulled it through the window. There was nothing much in the pockets — a pen-knife, pencil, handkerchief, and a pipe and pouch. Red opened the pouch and felt inside it. His hand came out holding a cablegram. It was from France, he saw, transmitted from an office in Calais. He looked at it quickly. It bore one word: TONIGHT.

Red stuffed it back in the pouch and replaced the coat. A whole lot of things were clearer to him now — now he could really go to work. That cable practically put the finishing touch to all his vague theories and suspicions. He'd give 'em enough rope and hope that they would hang themselves . . .

He hurried back to the stage and found Peter still holding the rest in conversation. 'Send for Lakeman?'

'Yes — Hallam phoned.'

'This is all intolerable,' Hallam burst out. 'Damn it, we can't keep the place open any longer with all these murders going on!'

'Don't make definite arrangements to close until tomorrow, at least, Mister

Hallam,' Red told him.

'What difference does it make whether I decide to close it down tonight or tomorrow?'

'A whole lot.'

'What do you mean, Mister Benton?'

'You'll see, Mister Hallam.'

There was a noise like a mighty, rushing wind, and Inspector Lakeman burst upon the scene, closely followed by Constable Hoskins. 'Now what?' he said furiously. 'Can't I have one peaceful minute? How can I search for Lestivoff when something's always happening here?'

'You couldn't have been searching in the right spots, Inspector,' said Red calmly, indicating the body.

'What . . . ? My God! Another corpse!'

Lakeman bent down with a grim expression on his face. When he rose he shook his head wearily. 'I wash my hands of it,' he said. 'In any case, they're sending two Yard men down in the morning, and bang goes my chance of promotion. But — ' he added, glancing round. 'Where the devil is Dawson?'

'Dawson?'

'Yes. I didn't relieve him of his duties. He should still be on the spot.'

'I saw him not an hour ago,' put in Hallam. 'He appeared to be going in the direction of the dressing rooms.'

'What? What the devil does he mean by not staying at his post? Why, damnit, he might have seen who cut that rope if he'd been on the job! Where is the dunderhead?'

One of the stage hands was dispatched to see if he could find PC Dawson. He returned in a short time, a sleepy-eyed constable tagging along behind him.

'Fahnd 'im in the dressin' rooms,' explained the man. 'Sahnd asleep, 'e was!'

'D — Did you wug — want me, Inspector?' said Dawson. 'I'm sorry. I happened to be looking round in the course of me duties like, and I went in this here dressing room, like, and saw a chair there. I thought I'd just sit down a bit, like, as I'd got that tired hanging round all day, like, and then . . .'

'You went to sleep, like?' sneered Lakeman.

Dawson hung his head. 'I expect I did,

Inspector. Just dropped off, like.'

'If you're not very careful you'll be just dropped off the force, *like*, my lad,' Lakeman grunted. 'In future, when I want anything doing, I'll give it to Hoskins here!'

Dawson seemed to be on the verge of tears, and Hoskins smiled a smug and superior smile.

'Blessed if there's much to choose between you both,' snorted the inspector. 'I did think you had a bit more of the grey matter than Hoskins, but now I'm thinking you couldn't make a thimbleful between you!'

The smile faded from Hoskins's face.

'Look Inspector,' said Red. 'Before you go any further, will you let me have a word with you?'

'At a time like this?' roared Lakeman.

'Remember once before when you wouldn't listen to me?'

Lakeman cooled off noticeably. 'Right,' he said. 'I'll see you outside the stage door if you want a private talk.'

When they were outside, Red took the inspector persuasively by the coat lapel. 'Now listen,' he said gently. 'Will you agree not to kick up too much fuss right now? I mean just cart away the body, and cart away Hoskins and Dawson also. I think tonight will be the end of all this; and if I'm right, well, you can present a complete solution to the Yard men tomorrow — and also the killer.'

'Benton, if you know anything it's your duty to tell me . . .'

'But I'm not going to. You'd only barge about like a bull in a china shop and ruin the whole thing. You can trust me, Inspector. When the time comes, I promise that you'll be there — and you can grab all the credit . . . All I want you to do is to take yourself and your men away from the Granada . . . not too obviously mind, but as if you've decided to leave it all to the Yard men, and feel that you'll gain nothing by guarding the dump all night. Be ready down at the station — and have half a dozen good men ready too. Then, when the showdown comes, I'll see you're in on it! How about it, Inspector — you've got nothing to lose.'

'Only my job,' grunted Lakeman dubiously.

'Forget it! After tonight, if you do as I ask, they'll make you one of the big four. And you'll be off the case anyway when the Yard boys get here. Now — is it a go?'

Lakeman studied his shoe thoughtfully, then looked Red in the eyes for a minute. Finally he nodded. 'You win! I'll take a chance on you, Benton. What do you want me to do?'

'Good! First of all, send everyone in the theatre home — and let them see that you leave with them. Don't hang about the place — I'm relying on one of them to come back, but I'll be on the spot and I'll know just what to look for, and where to look for it. Then when you've done that, stand by at the station . . . '

'I'm a fool, but I'll do it,' said Lakeman.

'You won't regret it, Inspector — oh, when you go back in there, send Peter out to me, will you? And get the body moved, and the place emptied as soon as you can . . . '

8

Red and Peter turned along the front and began walking towards the Pavilion Hotel.

'Get this the first time, Pete,' Red told him. 'And see you get it right! I want you to hire the fastest motorboat you can get hold of, and the largest. When you've got it, take it along the coast to the headland just behind the Granada. It's pretty deep water right up to the rock there, so you should be able to moor it someplace — but out of sight, mind. There are plenty of fissures in the rock and I guess you won't have much trouble running it into one of them. Run it in so it's ready to come straight out again. When you've done that stay with it — and listen! And try to keep the door at the back of Granada in focus, even if you have to move a little way away from the boat. Don't make any noise, just sit tight and watch and listen. Watch the back door, and listen to the sea.

'The minute you see a light or signal from the rear of the Granada, or, the second you hear an engine out to sea, head for the police station and get hold of Lakeman and his boys. Make it as fast as possible, and then bring them through the stage door and down into the cellars. If the door leading down is locked, bust it open. You'll find one of two things — either myself with a nice little bunch of crooks — or nothing. If it's nothing, get down to the motor boat quickly and head straight out to the channel.

'Keep going and listen for the sound of another boat. When you hear it, make contact — but be careful! Also, tell Lakeman to come armed. You'd better be armed, too — I'll lend you a revolver when we get back to the hotel.' He looked questioningly at the excited composer.

'Rely on me, Red,' said Peter. 'I'm glad we're getting down to business at last.'

'I will rely on you — but it may prove to be a sticky business. I'd have left it to the inspector, but he'd probably have had a squad of policemen trampling all over the place, and the birds would have spread their wings and left the nest. If all goes right, we'll get them red-handed — a nice bag. But everything depends on timing. Don't forget — the second you notice anything fishy, go for the inspector!'

'I won't let you down!'

'Good man! I imagine nothing will happen until it's fairly dark, but that's only in about another hour or so — they couldn't move before then because of the coastguard stations. In fact, it may not happen until well after midnight. In which case it'll be a long and chilly wait for you, Pete, so you'd better take a coat. But somehow I think it will happen before midnight. The cable said tonight.'

'Which cable?'

'I'll tell you about that later.'

They had reached the hotel and Red made straight for the bar. He scanned the drinkers gathered there, but Happy was nowhere to be seen. He crossed to the barman and said: 'Clancy, have you seen Mister Harringay? Has he been in here?'

'Not since he was in here with you this morning, sir.'

'Thanks, Clancy.'

He turned out of the bar into the dining room and stopped one of the waiters. 'Have you seen a short, tubby man with a shortage of hair and a bowler hat? You'd know him by the fact that he never surrenders the hat — always lays it by him on the table when he's eating?'

'You mean the gentleman who generally takes his meals with you, sir? No, I haven't seen him at all today.'

Red, followed by Peter, went up the stairs into his rooms, then into Happy's. There was no sign of Mister Harringay in either. He went downstairs, over to the desk clerk.

'Has Mister Harringay left any message for me?'

'No, sir. It would have been here in the rack if he had.'

'Thanks!'

He returned upstairs, extracted three revolvers from his case, loaded them, slipped two into his own pockets, and gave one to Peter. 'Look,' he said. 'I'm afraid I've let Happy in for a lot of trouble — possibly he's already had it. I should

71

never have allowed him to go down into the cellars alone . . . but anyway, I'll have to speed things up from here on. Go and get that boat now, Pete. Then do just as I told you.'

'Are you sure someone shouldn't stick with you? In case *you* run into trouble?'

'No. I'd sooner play it alone — I always have. Besides, you'll be more use getting that boat — we may need it.'

'But . . . but where are you going?'

'The Granada,' replied Red. 'So long for now, Pete!'

Peter watched him stride out for the concert hall again, then hurried away himself, clutching the revolver in his pocket.

Lakeman had kept his word: the Granada was locked and deserted. But that did not deter Red. While at the hotel he had supplied himself with his spare set of master keys, and within two minutes he had the door open and was inside the deserted building. Cautiously, he trod across the platform, down the steps, past the dressing rooms.

The door at the head of the cellar steps

was closed and locked, and the keys came into play again. It slid open quietly, as if the hinges had been kept regularly oiled. Red felt his way down the steps, torch in one hand, revolver in the other. He was alert for every sound, but there was none to hear.

On the last step he halted, brought the revolver up, flashed on the torch and swiveled it quickly round the cellars.

He had not expected them to be entirely deserted, but they were. Still quietly, he moved to the centre of the floor and shone his torch on all the old junk lying about. He began a methodical search, peering behind everything which could have concealed a man, ready to shoot on the instant. When he had covered the whole of the cellars and had looked at the back of everything bar some pieces of scenery which were flat up to the wall, he paused and scratched his head.

He couldn't be wrong! Surely he couldn't? Or had they got the wind up and called it off for tonight?

He stiffened. There was a scratching at

the back door, as if a key was being fitted into the lock. Red tensed, clicked off his light, and drew back to a corner.

The door opened and a dark figure showed against the skyline. It entered, closed the door behind it, and began to move towards the centre of the floor.

Red shifted his position slightly, unwisely. His moving foot knocked against an empty crate of some sort. From the darkness came the voice of the man who had entered: 'Waring? Is that you?'

'It's me,' said Red. He stepped forward, switching on the torch, outlining the man in a beam of silver. The man drew back with a curse. 'Don't move, brother, you're covered!' snapped Red warningly.

'Who — who are you?'

'That doesn't matter a lot. The point is, where are Waring and my assistant?'

'I don't know what you're talking about. Waring who? Who's your assistant? Who are you?'

'Benton's the name, and you can cut out the innocent act. I suspected this all along.'

'You're Benton? Benton the detective?

Then you must know I'm the caretaker here. I came to have a look round, see if everything was all right.'

'What funny story is this you're giving me?'

'It's true. I thought I'd better keep an eye on the place after all the funny tricks that have been going on . . . '

'Cut it out, mister. You're the only funny trick here. And you won't be funny for so long unless you talk. Where's Happy Harringay . . . if anything's happened to him, you're going to wish you'd lost your life in that accident you once had, instead of just three fingers! Come on, talk!'

'I tell you, I came to have a look round.'

'And sneaked in at the back door, and called out for Waring? Please, brother! I wasn't born yesterday!'

'Weren't you?' said the caretaker, and his voice was changed. Now there was exultation in it, and Red was on his guard.

'Come on,' he snarled. 'Where's Harringay? Where's Waring?'

'I believe Waring is right behind you, Mister Benton!'

'Don't give me that old line. I'm not looking away and giving you the chance too . . . Ugh!'

Something descended with smashing force on Red's neck and head.

Waring *was* behind him . . .

9

When Red regained consciousness there was a throbbing pain at the base of his skull. His mouth felt hot and dry, and a dim light was searing its way into his eyeballs. He opened his eyes and glanced around. At least he wasn't dead yet, and while there was life . . .

He was in a small chamber, no more than six feet square and five high. On the left was a small door which was now open, and Red could see it led into the cellars. It suddenly struck him what a fool he had been not to move that flat scenery and look for just such a door!

Apparently this was where Waring had been in hiding and, while Red had been menacing the caretaker, he had slipped out and sneaked up behind Red with some sort of weapon.

Waring and Lipton, the caretaker, were seated on upturned boxes, smoking. Waring was a large, fat, sallow man, with shifty eyes and a pasty complexion. Red could easily picture him in the role of blackmailer and murderer — the eyes were cruel and cunning.

Red became aware of someone lying beside him. A voice said: 'Jeez! It's you, Borss! I never thought I'd see youse again!'

Happy was also bound. There was a nasty cut on his forehead, a trickle of dried blood running from it down to his chin. Red grinned at him and twisted half over.

'What happened?'

'I got down here like youse told me, Chief, an' I was mighty quiet. I kinda figured I oughta find myself a hidey hole, so I gets behind a piece of scenery which is propped against de wall.

'I am squatting there, looking inta the cellar, when *wham*, something hits me over the turnip from behind, an' I goes out like a light. When I wakes up, here I am! An' this guy with the pale puss, he's here too — in fact, by all accounts he is the very guy which whammed me. He hangs about here for ages, then we hears

78

voices from the cellar. I am going to yell out, when this monkey moseys over again, and before I can put up a squawk he socks me again. Then I don't see nothin' but comets until I come round an' find you here with me, you havin' had a touch of the sleepin' draft also!'

'Tough luck, Happy. If I'd known more this morning, I wouldn't have sent you down here. No use moaning over it, anyway.' Red broke off and looked up. Waring and Lipton were coming across to them. Lipton was grinning, but Waring's eyes were uneasy.

'So you woke up, did you? You were a bit too clever this time, Benton!' sneered the caretaker.

'Maybe I was.'

'Much too clever, in fact. Do you know what we're going to do with you and your friend?'

'I could make a guess! But it won't do you any good, Lipton. Your racket's all washed up. It was a good gag while it lasted, and I guess you made plenty on it. Clever of you to think of smuggling wanted criminals out of England, and this place is ideal for it. What made you think of it in the first place?'

'I'll tell you that, Mister Benton. After I had that accident, my life was ruined. I had been used to getting all the money I could ever need from my playing — but I spent it all and never thought of the future. When I lost my fingers and had to give up my work, they gave me this job here as caretaker — two pounds ten a week, Mister Benton, after I had been used to a hundred! Do you wonder that I was bitter? Where were all the friends on whom I had spent my money? Friends? Bah! Swine, that's what they were! They never came near!

'Perhaps I brooded on my injuries, Mister Benton. I don't know. Perhaps I always had something of the lawless in me. Whatever it was, when a couple of gentlemen across the channel approached me and suggested that the old Granada was an ideal place for smuggling contraband into the country, I agreed instantly. That was how it started. I handled the stuff on this side for them — drugs, silks, brandy, anything which would bring money. Very profitable it was, too. Then a man who had taken drugs from me and sold them to his clientele got into trouble. He came to me and asked if I could smuggle him out of the country. He offered five hundred pounds. I saw no reason why he should not travel back on the boat which brought the smuggled goods. So I entrusted him to my good friends, Pierre and Jean. From then on, Mister Benton, we had a regular business with these wanted men. You know how news travels fast in the underworld.'

'And when they decided to reopen the Granada, you didn't like the idea! If it had proved successful, you wouldn't have been able to carry on with your little games. So you started murdering people, trying to give the place a bad name, trying to scare away the audiences. And you almost succeeded — but not quite!' Red concluded.

'No, alas, not quite. I went a little too far. I realized that tonight. Instead of frightening attention away from the Granada, I focused attention on it! That is why I shall have to leave on the boat tonight with Mister Waring. But I have a nice little fortune to take with me, Mister Benton!' Lipton patted the suitcase beside him. 'Of course, now that you have been so clever, I fear we will have to take you with us, Mister Benton. You and your assistant. But only as far as mid-channel. And if you can swim home from there, bound and weighted, you will deserve your freedom!'

'I suppose it was you who killed Lestivoff?'

'Yes, I must take the credit for that. After you had all left, I turned back again. Lestivoff didn't suspect, and before he knew anything I had knocked him senseless. I'm afraid I had to make sure he was dead by hitting him repeatedly on the back of the head with my iron bar — then I hoisted him into the curtain, and when the time came I cut the rope — it was rather a good effect, don't you think?'

'One of these days you're going to have something in common with Lestivoff! You'll be dangling on the end of a rope yourself! But in your case, nobody's going to cut it! At least, not until you're good and dead!'

'I think not,' smiled the caretaker. 'They don't hang men in France, Mister Benton. Madame Guillotine has the honor there.'

'You're not going to reach France, Lipton — take my word on that.'

'What does he mean?' gasped Waring, speaking for the first time.

'Bah! He's bluffing, trying to get us rattled — aren't you, Mister Benton?'

Red ignored him and turned to Waring. 'You're pretty stupid, Waring.' He smiled. 'Do you know that the first murder was committed with your revolver?'

'Yes, he knows that,' interrupted Lipton. 'I didn't happen to have my own.'

'I told you not to use that gun,' gulped Waring. 'I knew they'd trace it to me!'

'What does it matter? You're wanted already for murder. And in any event, you will be safe by midnight.'

Waring nodded and went back to his seat. Lipton stood watching the two prisoners reflectively. Then he smiled. 'No, I shan't bother you two gentlemen now,' he said. 'After all, you have the right to spend your last moments in peace.' He returned to Waring's side and the two sat smoking.

'Gee, Borss,' murmured Happy, 'it sure looks like we came to the end of the trail! I wonder where my pore old maw is tonight?'

'Don't take it to heart, Happy,' whispered Red softly. 'You don't think I walked down here without preparing, do you?'

Happy glanced at him suddenly, eyes wide, but Red pursed his lips, and the unhappy Mister Harringay heeded the warning.

'Damn it,' exploded Waring suddenly. 'How much longer do we have to wait? After staying here for weeks, the place is driving me mad! When will they come?'

'Have patience, my friend,' said Lipton. 'They will be here on time, you needn't worry about that.' He looked at his watch. 'It is now almost eleven fifteen — they should be here in fifteen minutes.'

The fifteen minutes seemed to crawl by. Red tried to struggle free from his bonds, but the watchful caretaker spotted him, and came and aimed a crushing kick at his stomach.

'That,' he said, as Red squirmed and struggled for breath, 'will serve to distract your attention from other things!'

'You fingerless little rat,' growled Happy. 'I'll moider youse if I get my hands free . . . '

Lipton looked at his watch again, then he picked up a red lantern from the corner and lit it. He stepped out into the cellar and made for the rear door. He opened it about halfway, stood back in the middle of the cellar, and waved the lantern to and fro three times. Red judged that this was the 'come ahead' signal, signifying that all was OK. The lantern, being well back in the cellar, would not be seen by anyone on the beach or cliffs, but only by those out to sea and in more or less direct line with the partly opened door. But what Lipton did not know was that if Peter had obeyed his instructions, it had been seen by him also, and he was now on his way to the station to pick up Lakeman and the rest.

'They should be here in about ten minutes now,' Lipton said, and an air of tense expectancy fell on the occupants of the cellar.

★　★　★

It had been a long, cold wait for Peter. He had hired the boat and taken up his position between two out-jutting rocks, not a stone's throw from the stone steps which led up to the Granada. At some risk to life and limb, he had climbed to the summit of the rock nearest to the concert hall, and had found that he was able to see the shadowy back of the Granada from his present position. Darkness had crept up on to the spot he imagined the rear door to be. At the same time, remembering Red's instructions, he listened intently to the sounds from the channel, but heard nothing more than occasional cry from some passing bird.

After a wait of what seemed hours, he judged it must be close on midnight, and glanced at his watch, wondering if Red had made a blunder in his assumptions.

To his surprise it was only eleven twenty-five, and he shivered and drew his coat closer about him.

Minutes crawled by, then far out he thought he heard a soft *put-put-put* from the darkness. He stiffened and listened again, but it had stopped. Would that be the boat Red had meant, or was he imagining things? Had his overwrought nerves conjured up in his mind the sound he had been waiting for, or was there actually a boat out there?

As he crouched there undecided, from the direction of the Granada came a sudden dim glow of red light! He could discern an oblong streak, lighter than the surrounding gloom, and as he watched the red glow moved across this space three times.

That was it! That clinched things! He'd better get moving — now! Recklessly, he clambered across the rock, down the opposite side. The rocks were frequent here and, skipping agilely from one to the other, he managed to reach the mainland without mishap. Here another risky climb, and when he reached the flat top he heaved a sigh of relief.

Without pausing, he began running to the station.

Wild and disheveled, he burst in on Inspector Lakeman, Constables Hoskins and Dawson, and three other members of the force. They were seated round the small desk, drinking hot tea and waiting.

'Is this it?' barked Lakeman. He was on his feet, reaching out for his hat, before Peter had had a chance to speak.

Peter nodded. 'Back to the Granada,' he said. 'Those were Red's instructions. He's there himself!'

'What's happened?' demanded Lakeman, quickly marshalling his men.

'I've no idea — we'll probably find out when we get there!'

Within two minutes they started off at a rapid run for the concert hall. Peter and Lakeman were in the lead, both armed with revolvers. Behind them came the constables, armed with heavy truncheons and handcuffs.

They made good time, and less than eighteen minutes after Peter had seen the red light, they were entering the silent building. Their torches cut through the gloom, but there was nothing to be seen on the platform. Peter followed instructions and led them straight to the cellar door. It was unlocked, exactly as Red had left it when he had entered earlier.

Lakeman and Peter flung themselves down the stairs, the stalwarts of the law close behind them. The cellar was brightened by the glow from four torches and the contents were thrown into brilliant clarity.

But they had drawn blank. The place was deserted.

'Now what?' grunted Lakeman, turning to Peter.

'He said there might possibly be no one here — now I've got to take the boat and put out into the channel.'

'Boat?'

'Yes, a fast motorboat which I hired and moored near the bottom of the steps. I think we can get to it that way.'

The party pushed through the open cellar door and into the night. One at a time they half-ran, half-stumbled down the steps leading to the bottom of the headland. As Peter had thought, they were able to reach the boat by means of a narrow ledge which ran along just above the sea. But at the point of rock behind which the boat was moored, there was a nasty jump of some four feet. Peter took it in his stride, but Lakeman, whose athletic days were long over, landed squarely in the middle of six feet of extremely damp and chilly water. Sundry grunts and curses emanated from the darkness, but the inspector quickly pulled himself to dry rock and followed onto the boat. The PCs, all younger men, managed the jump without accident, and the full party piled into the waiting boat. She was tuned up and ready to go, and Peter started the motor and tore out of the cove. Inspector Lakeman, who had been standing up shouting orders, pitched backwards on his men as they took to the sea at top speed.

Peter obeyed Red's instructions and drove straight out into the channel. They had covered a good distance when he suddenly stopped the motor, and the boatload of men were silent, listening.

Then, from their right and quite close, came the sound of an engine starting up.

'Over to the right and slightly forward!' shouted Lakeman, and Peter brought the motor to life again and swung in the direction of the other craft.

10

After Lipton had signalled with the lantern, he reclosed the door. He put the extinguished lantern back in its corner and returned to the cellar. 'We had better be getting ready to go, Waring,' he said. 'If you will help me to carry our two friends into the cellar.'

They seized Red roughly, carried him into the cellar and threw him against the wall. Then Happy. Then Lipton brought his suitcase, and everything was ready.

Waring apparently had no personal possessions with him. He was showing signs of relief and excitement at the prospect of getting to the continent, where he would be more or less a free man again, provided he kept under cover to a certain extent.

Minutes passed. Red fell to wondering if Peter had fulfilled his part of the plan, and found himself fervently hoping he had. If so, he would be just about nearing the police station now.

It had been Red's plan to capture Lipton and Waring, then wait for the Frenchmen from the boat and catch them also. He had hoped to have a complete bag for Lakeman. Unfortunately, things had failed to work out just right, and now he himself was an unarmed prisoner. But as long as Peter played his hand right, nothing could go wrong — except that Red and Happy might well be under fathoms of water before the others could help them.

That was a chance that had to be taken — one of the risks of playing a lone hand.

There was a gentle knock on the cellar door, repeated four times. Lipton stepped forward and opened it. The man who entered was burly and bull-necked. He had popping frog-like eyes, and an unkempt beard which hung down over the roll collar of a seaman's jersey. A pair of rough corduroys and a knee-length pair of sea boots completed the picture. Pulled down on his massive head was an old yachting cap, and under one arm he carried a large bundle wrapped in oil silk.

'Pierre!' exclaimed Lipton, stepping forward. 'Good to see you again!'

'*Oui*,' grunted Pierre, then indicated Waring and the two captives. 'What ees all thees, Michael?'

'There isn't time to explain at the moment. Enough to say the game's up, and I'll have to clear out myself. This man is Waring — he has paid for passage to France in the usual way. These two are getting free passage, but only as far as mid-channel. There we shall have to part company with them, I fear.'

Pierre was blinking rapidly, trying to assimilate all that his accomplice was telling him. One point he grasped thoroughly.

'You mean that ze smuggling can no longer take place? But I 'ave brought ze packet of drugs over . . . I am desolate! What shall I now do?'

'We'll have to take them back. I expect we'll be able to find another base suitable for smuggling stuff in, at some time in the near future. But at present the Granada is too warm — that's why it is imperative for me to leave with you tonight.'

'As you will,' assented Pierre. 'But Jean,

he will be very angry with all thees.'

'I'll explain to him — I suppose you left him to watch the boat?'

Pierre nodded. 'I followed our usual plan. We stop ze launch well out and here I come in ze small rowing boat, as always.'

'Do you think there'll be room for the four of us in it? I don't want to leave these two here to rouse suspicions. I want to make a clean getaway, and if they were found murdered in the cellar there would certainly be a lot of fuss.'

'We will make room.'

Pierre dropped his bundle, crossed to Happy and, picking him up, slung him over one shoulder like a sack of coke. Lipton picked up his case and the bundle of drugs, and motioned to Waring to get hold of Red. Waring did so, and the small party passed from the cellar and down onto the steps leading to the rowing boat.

The boat was tied to a rock on the shingle, bobbing up and down in the shallow water. Happy and Red were slung into it, and then the three crooks piled in also. The boat sank perilously low in the water, until the slightest movement swilled the sea over the gunwale.

Pierre cast off and seized an oar, handing the other one to Waring. Both men started rowing; but Waring, unused to such an art, did nothing but catch crabs. Lipton ripped the oar from him with an oath and started rowing himself. Slowly, the boat pulled away from the headland and made straight out to mid-channel.

'How far out is Jean?' demanded Lipton.

'He ees about five minutes only. The launch, she is ready to go the minute I return.'

They pulled away in silence.

Neither of them noticed Red. But Red was extremely busy in the end of the boat. When he had been pitched in he had felt something hard strike his back; on closer investigation it had resolved itself to be a boat-hook with sharp, rusty prongs. Red's hands had been tied behind his back and he was now busily engaged sawing his bonds up and down this Heaven-sent means of escape. Once or twice he misjudged and the sharp iron bit into his flesh; but grimly he stuck to it, feeling more and more satisfied with every parted strand.

'What is that?' demanded Waring suddenly.

Everyone glanced back towards the headland. Up there, in the inkiness of the night, lights were bobbing about. Lipton peered incredulously, then his teeth clenched.

'Whoever it is, they are coming down the steps. But it's all right — they can't follow without a boat.' Nevertheless, he began to pull more strongly, and once or twice he glanced evilly at Red.

'We should be near now,' said Pierre, and he paused and gave a low whistle. From the left came an answering whistle. Waring operated the rudder and the two oarsmen pulled again.

'Listen!' said Lipton suddenly.

From the direction they had left came the sudden roar of a motor. It echoed across the water, seeming to gather volume each second.

'Someone is after us,' gasped Waring. 'For God's sake, pull for the launch!'

With renewed vigor, the two men hauled at the oars, and a dark shape appeared before them.

Jean was leaning over the side of the trim motor launch. He was dressed much as Pierre was, but he was smaller and had a wizened face. As the three crooks lifted Red and Happy aboard, Lipton gave a brief explanation to him, and Jean seemed annoyed.

'So there is someone after us, you fool!' he grated. 'Why did you not stop us coming when there is all this trouble?'

'It's no use arguing,' panted Lipton. 'Just start the boat at once and let's get away.'

The sound of the other boat was now incredibly close, and suddenly the engine was cut off.

At the same instant the launch's engines roared into life and the sleek craft cut through the water towards the French coast. Red listened intently for the other boat, but the sound of their own engines drowned the noise it made. Something told him that this launch could move — unless it could be halted, the rescuers might be too late . . .

'Get rid of those two!' shouted Pierre from the wheel.

Lipton hurried over with a length of chain, and bent over Red. Red pulled mightily on his partly frayed bonds and had the pleasure of feeling them snap apart. He came lunging up from the deck, his head crashing home under Lipton's jawbone. Lipton pitched backwards, falling heavily against Pierre, knocking him from the wheel. Red leapt forward, grabbed the wheel, and gave it a mighty twist. The boat spun crazily in the current and swung broadside-on.

Pierre regained his feet and came flying at Red. Red ducked neatly, and the burly Frenchman shot over his back and landed with his head against the deck. Jean, armed with a boathook, came rushing forward. Red spun the wheel again, and the launch jolted sufficiently to put the little Frenchman off balance. Red caught the hook end of his weapon and jabbed it backwards towards Jean unexpectedly. The blunt handle smashed home on Jean's mouth and he let out a shrill yelp of agony, spitting out teeth and blood.

'Waring!' screamed Lipton, coming to his feet. 'Give us a hand, you fool!'

Waring had been sitting shivering until now, but at Lipton's cry he hurled himself at Red's legs. Red went down under the tackle, and Lipton, Waring and Jean piled on him. Pierre was crawling to his feet and, as the boat was still spinning wildly, he crossed to the wheel and took it again.

A bullet came whistling through the air close to his head. Strong beams of light flashed out, outlining the launch for the pursuers to see. Peter's boat was almost on top of them.

Lakeman was firing his revolver over the launch as a warning, but the crooks did not heed it. Jean and Lipton left Red to Waring. Lipton took the wheel and Pierre joined Jean at the stern. They produced revolvers and began firing back. There was a cry from the attacking boat. One of the policemen clutched his chest, coughed, and fell backwards into the water.

'Get Dawson, Hoskins!' rapped Lakeman. Hoskins slipped out of his boots and tunic and, without a word, plunged in after his rival.

The fight went on. Pierre suddenly

doubled up and slumped to the deck. Jean stooped, took the gun from his lifeless hand, and continued to fire. Then, with a curse, he pitched the two guns away.

'The guns are empty, Lipton!' he shouted. 'There is only one chance — this is a strong craft — *ram them*!'

'You fool,' replied Lipton. 'We'll all drown!'

'Ram them!' Jean staggered over to the wheel and pushed Lipton away with one hand. The caretaker stumbled and fell. Waring came to his feet with a yell of terror. Red came to his. Happy blinked at the scene dismally. Something told him he wasn't going to get the chance to inspect any Scotch distilleries. Jean swung the wheel with savage force and the launch swung round in a wide arc, her nose pointing towards the motorboat.

'They're going to ram us!' shouted Lakeman. 'Look out!'

Then the launch was on them, with a shattering, jarring impact. The motorboat caved in at the side. Lakeman and two or three of his men leaped onto the launch as it swung away. Jean and Waring had no time to fight back. The police used their

101

truncheons with considerable vigor and Waring and Jean went down under their onslaught. Meanwhile, at the other side of the small cabin, Lipton had pulled a gun from his pocket and levelled it at Red. His finger curled round the trigger.

But Happy, still bound, had seen what was afoot; and as the caretaker pulled the trigger, he rolled heavily forward and cannoned into the front of the man's legs. Lipton pitched forward, and the bullet he intended for Red ripped into the fleshy part of Happy's thigh. Then Red was coming forward, and Lipton was backing away, firing crazily towards the detective.

The rowing boat was still tied to the launch, and Lipton bent and slipped the mooring. With his suitcase of money in one hand and the gun in the other, he jumped recklessly into the small boat and shot away from the launch. He dropped gun and case and reached for the oars. Red plunged into the water and swam strongly after him. Lipton stood up in the boat, lashing savagely at Red's defenseless head. Red caught the side of the boat and hauled . . .

The boat wobbled violently and Lipton shot down into the water. He came up beside Red, clutched his coat, and felt his way up to Red's neck. His good hand wound into Red's neck, the fingers biting into the soft skin; his other hand came clawing towards Red's eyes. Red caught him by the chin and wound his legs round the caretaker's middle. Exerting all his strength, he held tight to the side of the boat, and with his other hand forced the crook's face underwater. The claw-like fingers ripped and tore at his neck but he held on grimly. Lipton got his teeth, underwater, to the hand which was pressing his face down . . . they sank into the fingers, biting to the bone . . .

Red groaned with the agony, relaxed his legs from the man's middle, and drove his knee forward into Lipton's groin with all the force the water would permit him. The biting stopped as Lipton gasped for air and received only water. Bubbles tore upwards from his tortured lungs. Gradually the grip on Red's throat relaxed.

Lipton began to sink and Red released him, letting him drop . . .

Red climbed into the boat. He opened Lipton's suitcase and began to stuff every available pocket in his clothes with notes. He considered he had earned it.

The launch was within hailing distance, the torches of the police denoting that they had gained the upper hand. Red rowed towards it and climbed aboard with the case. He handed it to Lakeman.

'What's this?' demanded the perspiring inspector.

'Lipton's money,' Red informed him with a grin. Lakeman glanced suspiciously towards the detective's bulging pockets, then he shrugged and smiled good-naturedly.

'How's Happy?' Red said anxiously. 'Is he all right?'

Lakeman nodded. 'Just a flesh wound — that man saved your life, Red.'

'I know — it isn't the first time, either. I'll have to reward him.'

'How?' asked Lakeman curiously.

'By taking him up to Scotland — he's got a date with a distillery,' grinned Red.

'We picked most of them up,' said the inspector. 'Dawson's shot through the lung, but he'll pull through, I fancy. The hefty French chap is dead, shot through the head. His partner is knocked silly and cuffed, and so is the other fellow.'

'The other fellow is Waring — Gillam Waring,' said Red.

'You don't tell me? My, won't I get a nice bit of promotion over this lot!' said Lakeman happily. 'Red, I take back all the things I said about you when you came down here!'

'Thanks! Lipton's dead too — he seemed to get his throat mixed up with some water,' Red explained.

A shape loomed up through the darkness. 'Ahoy there,' called a voice. 'Has anything been happening?'

'Who's that?' called the inspector.

'Coastguard cutter. We thought we heard shots and a crash from the lookout, so we came to investigate. What have you been up to?'

'Nothing, nothing at all,' called Red cheerfully. 'We've just been having a bit of a regatta, that's all!'

★ ★ ★

England was thrilled by the revelations of the CONCERTO CASE, as the newspapers called it.

Inspector Lakeman, now a chief inspector, was held up as an example of what policemen should be. For him the adventure was complete.

Peter Innis played his 'Concerto for Fear' right through, and soon afterwards played it to vast crowds at the Albert Hall. His future father-in-law gave his blessings to the wedding and preparations were rushed through.

Waring dangled from the end of a rope one cold morning at eight o'clock.

Jean went to prison for quite a long time.

Lipton fed the fishes for days.

The Granada Palace Concert Hall boomed.

Happy, after two weeks in hospital without a drop, went to Scotland with Red and kept his date with the distillery.

Red found that he had benefited to the tune of almost a thousand pounds from Lipton's suitcase.

★ ★ ★

Red Benton reclined behind his desk, smoking contentedly, his feet stuck up on the polished woodwork. The door opened, and Happy Harringay made his entrance.

'A dame to see you'se, Borss.'

Red pursed his lips. He was attired in a morning suit and carnation for the part he was shortly to play. He really had little time to spare for his visitor. 'What's she like, Happy?'

She's the bee's knees, borss! You know her — it's the Pelham-Davis dame.'

Red looked interested and sat up. 'OK. Shoot her in!'

Mavis Pelham-Davis shimmied into the office. She came across to a chair, sat down in it, and crossed her legs. Red admired the turn of her ankles, the sheer silk stockings and the provocative roundness of her knees.

'You wanted to see me?' he enquired.

'I did, rather. You've forgotten to send in your bill, Mister Benton,' she said in a soft, musical voice.

'Forget it! Let's say the retainer you paid covered the case, shall we?'

'But you said your fee was very high?'

'Sure — but the case wasn't so difficult. Besides, I was able to do another little job while I was down there, which paid me well. So I really don't think you owe me much.'

'Did you have much trouble finding Waring?' she said.

Red grinned. 'Why not forget it?'

'Oh, but Mister Benton! You can't just put me off like that! I want to know all about it!'

'You can't right now. I'm due to act as best man at Peter Innis's wedding. But maybe we could meet tonight at my flat for supper?'

She stood up, her face cold. 'No thank you, Mister Benton. In that case I'll do without knowing. Please let me pay what I owe and I won't trouble you any more.'

'I said forget it.'

'I would prefer to settle up, if you don't mind. What do I owe?'

Red stood up, came round the desk, and faced her. She stood quite still as his arm went round her waist. 'This!' he said, and bending forward he kissed her full on the lips.

She made no effort to pull away, but stood there, neither resenting nor returning the embrace. Red drew away, grinning at her flushed face.

'Go ahead,' he said mockingly. 'Slap my face, why don't you?'

For a moment she stood there breathing hard. Then she turned and walked towards the door. She opened it, turned round and stared back. 'You're rather presumptuous, aren't you?'

Red shrugged his shoulders. 'You insisted on paying what you owed me.'

'And I suppose I should think your services cheap at the price of a kiss?'

'Think what you like, sister,' he said shortly. He turned to his desk and rooted amongst his papers, expecting to hear the door slam.

'I suppose because you're a private detective you think you have the right to insult somebody you hardly know by suggesting supper in your flat?' she said.

'Aren't you going?' said Red patiently.

'I certainly am! But, Red . . . ' she turned sharply. Her tone had altered. Her eyes were shining.

'What?' he said.

'What's the address?' she said softly. 'And what time shall I see you . . . ?'

Death Flows
Down River

1

Red Benton leaned back in his office chair and nodded to the man who had just entered his comfortable office. 'Find yourself a chair, Gregor.' He smiled. 'And let's hear what brings you round to my office this bright May morning.'

Detective Inspector Gregor of the London police force plumped wearily into a chair, threw his hat on the desk and brought out the foul-smelling pipe he affected.

'You going to smoke that?' enquired Red.

The Yard man nodded.

'Just a second, then.' Red pressed a button on his desk, the door opened and Happy Harringay, his American assistant, entered. 'Happy,' said Red solemnly, 'would you mind opening all the windows — Gregor's going to smoke his pipe.'

The detective scowled and replaced his pipe in his pocket.

'All right, Happy,' said Red. 'He's going to spare us after all.'

'OK, Borss,' said Mister Harringay, and withdrew.

'Look here, Benton,' snapped the inspector. 'I didn't come here to be made a fool of! I came — well — that is, I . . . '

'I know.' Red smiled. 'You dropped in to ask what I think about the unusual accidents which have been happening lately. You dropped in because Spinnerton told you he intended to retain me to find out exactly what happened to his daughter — isn't that it?'

'Yes, that's it, Benton. You know the case?'

'Only the little I read in the papers — and that didn't tell me much.'

'Well then, it's this way. The first body was found about two months ago. It came floating down the Thames and it was in a damned bad shape. It had been cut and mutilated in a horrible manner, particularly about the stomach. It was the body of a tramp. We couldn't identify him or trace any living relatives. Of course, we got on the case right away.'

'But the papers said it was an accident.'

'It wasn't. It was murder, Benton! We gave the reporters the idea that we thought it was an accident, to lull whoever had done it into a sense of false security while we conducted our investigation. And we were still in the middle of that investigation when the second body was found!'

'Only this time there was more fuss . . . '

'There was a lot of fuss! When the daughter of Lord Spinnerton is found floating down the Thames in a nasty condition, somebody — in fact, everybody — wants to know just why. Especially his Lordship. It was no use telling him it was another accident. And some of the reporters thought it a bit funny that two bodies, both in a similar state, should be found floating down the river within a matter of two months of each other. But we managed to persuade them that it would be best to hush things up for the time being. We're doing our best on the case, and I can't imagine why Lord Spinnerton should come to *you*.'

'Possibly,' said Red, lighting a cigarette, 'because he wants the case solved. I've accepted his retainer — he's paying me one thousand pounds for taking the case. That's a bit more than the Yard pay you, Gregor.'

Gregor scowled again. 'I'll admit you're damn lucky,' agreed Gregor. 'And I think it likely that you may find out more than us.'

'Very likely,' Red agreed.

'But then, you don't have to tackle these things from the routine angle. We do.'

'I know, I know, but you didn't come down here to tell me that. Come to the point, Inspector.'

'*Detective* Inspector,' growled Gregor. Red's habit of dropping the 'detective' part always annoyed Gregor. 'The point is this: will you cooperate?'

'I always have done, haven't I?'

'When it's been to your own advantage, Benton. I know you. I know you only think of money — how much money you can make on this and that and the other. To you, a case spells nothing more than pounds, shillings and pence.'

'Skip the shillings and pence,' said Red. 'You're thinking of *your* wage packet now, Gregor. To me a case just spells *pounds* — and plenty of 'em.'

'That's the trouble with you! You don't give a damn who gets murdered, provided there's money in it for you!'

'You can cut that line, Gregor,' drawled Red. 'I know it all. Just remember that I'm a private detective, not a sentimentalist. If I shed a tear for every guy and dame in the world who gets killed, I'd be able to supply half of London with a handy reservoir.'

Gregor tapped his foot on the floor and settled his plump person more firmly on the chair. 'What I want to know is, are you working with us?'

Red reflected for a moment, then shook his head. 'No,' he said. 'As ever, I am working alone. At the same time, if I can help you along I will do — and I'll let you take the credit for the pinch. That's fair enough.'

'Very well, if you won't cooperate all along the line I suppose I'll have to be content with that.'

'You will,' Red agreed. Gregor rose from his seat and grabbed his hat. Red also stood up, crossed to the hat stand in the corner, and put on a dirty-looking raincoat and a shabby trilby.

'Where the devil are you going?' demanded the inspector.

'With you,' Red informed him politely and persuasively. 'I want to see the body. Where is it?'

'Do you think I'm going out of my way to take you down to the morgue to see the body? You're wrong, Benton, you're dead wrong!'

'Tut, tut, Inspector!' said Red, scandalized. 'Speaking like that after asking me to cooperate! I am surprised!'

'Surprised or not,' said Gregor, with emphasis. 'I am not taking you to the morgue.'

★　★　★

'Well, here we are,' said Gregor, fifteen minutes later as they strode up the steps leading to the morgue. 'They brought

Dalia Spinnerton in last night, about an hour after she'd been found.'

The attendant came from behind his desk and touched his cap to the inspector. ''ow d'yer do, sir. Who'djer wanter see this time?'

'The stiff they brought in last night, Fred,' Gregor told him.

The attendant led them along a passage, down a short flight of stone steps, and into the refrigerating chamber.

'All this dead meat,' observed Red, glancing round. 'All nice and fresh — and England rationed!'

'You've a lousy sense of humour, Benton,' grunted Gregor. They had halted by a white slab on which was a sheeted figure. Fred whipped the sheet away and the corpse was revealed. Even Red, tough as he undoubtedly was, felt a little sick at the sight he saw.

The dead girl had been a good looker, no getting away from it. What was left of her figure was exquisite: shapely, tiny feet; well-rounded limbs; slender waist. Her hair was an attractive auburn shade, and although it was now lank and bedraggled through the dead girl's immersion in the water, Red could see it must have been very attractive when coiffured. The girl's features were small and pert; her nose line spoke of breeding, her forehead of intelligence and sophistication. She was nude.

'Was she picked up like this?' asked Red.

'Exactly — not a stitch on her.'

'And was the other corpse — the tramp — was he naked?'

'As the day he was born,' said Gregor.

'Then how the hell,' said Red, 'did you know he was a tramp?'

The inspector smiled. 'Easy. We have got brains, Benton, although you may not think so. The fact that he was unshaven, that the doctor stated he hadn't eaten for some time before the murder, and that his fingernails were uncared for and his hair badly needed trimming — that and the fact that we couldn't trace him as being a missing person.'

'That isn't conclusive proof,' said Red.

'Why not?'

'Well, suppose he'd been kept prisoner

before the murder was committed? Say for a few weeks. That would account for his hair, his nails, and his lack of a shave.'

'But it wouldn't account for his feet. They were the feet of a man who is used to walking a lot.'

'Be your age, Gregor,' drawled Red. 'Postmen walk a lot, so do commercial travelers. So do dozens of other guys in various jobs. But allowing that he was a tramp, was he cut in the same way as this girl?' He indicated the girl's stomach. It was ripped and torn open, not jaggedly, but cleanly, as if some surgical instrument had been used on it.

Gregor nodded.

'What did the surgeon have to say about all this?'

'Very little. He said that it seemed to have been cut with a scalpel, or something like that. He couldn't tell why the incisions had been made — said they were most irregular and could hardly have been done with any definite purpose in view. Thought it was the work of a maniac, a second Jack the Ripper.'

Red knitted his brow and drew the

sheet up again. 'It could be — but why is only the stomach cut? Why not some other part of the body?'

Gregor shook his head.

Red threw the sheet over the body again, turned towards the exit. 'By the way,' he said, 'is it all right for me to bring Sir Arthur Playmer to see the body?'

'You mean the famous surgeon? Sure, go ahead. Bring the entire medical profession if you like — but you're wasting your time.'

2

Red Benton strolled easily down Harley Street, noted the name on a brass plate outside a door, and turned in. He found himself in a reception room. A pretty, blonde-haired nurse with very red lips was seated behind a desk, neat and trim in a white uniform. She glanced up as Red entered.

'I'd like to see Sir Arthur,' Red informed her.

'Have you an appointment, sir?' she asked, smiling.

'If I had I should have said so,' Red told her shortly. 'I don't need any appointment. Tell him a gent wishes to see him on a matter of grave importance, will you?'

'I'm sorry sir, but Sir Arthur is very busy — he will only see his regular patients without a set appointment. Now if you will leave your name — '

'The name is Benton — I don't suppose it will convey anything to him

— but let him hear it right now, sister, will you?'

The nurse looked at Red helplessly. He grinned good-naturedly and she smiled and said: 'Very well, Mister Benton. You're a very determined man and you seem quite sure of yourself. I'll let Sir Arthur know you're here.' She depressed a lever on the desk and spoke into a small microphone. 'There is a gentleman called Mister Benton to see you, sir. He says it is on a matter of grave importance.'

'Tell him I can't see him at the moment — he must phone for an appointment,' came back the voice of the famous surgeon. The blonde nurse flipped up the lever again.

'You heard, sir?'

'Yep, I heard. But heeded not. Where is Sir Arthur?'

She shook her head, but he saw her eyes flicker to a room on the right, bearing the words 'Consulting Room.'

Red grinned again. 'I think I'll drop in on the great man,' he told the nurse. 'Regardless of phoning for an appointment.'

'Oh but you can't, Mister Benton. I'm not allowed to let you go past this desk.'

'Is that so? And what, my lovely, will you do if I attempt to go past? How do you propose to stop me, may I ask?'

She looked considerably agitated. 'I couldn't stop you — but I could call a policeman.'

'Skip it,' Red told her. 'I'm a policeman, so that wouldn't get you anywhere.'

Her eyes had widened. 'You're a policeman? Oh, in that case I am sure Sir Arthur would stretch a point and see you, sir. I will ask him again if you can show me your pass or some means of identification. I take it policemen carry something to prove who they are?'

'Don't bother,' Red said. 'I'll just go right in.' He came round the desk and the girl jumped up rapidly and stood in front of the door to the consulting room.

'I'm sorry . . . ' she began, then she stopped and gave a small gasp, for Red had taken her firmly round the waist and had lifted her gently aside.

'You're a nice kid,' smiled Red. 'But you mustn't start trying conclusions with us tough guys.' And with another sweet smile, he had opened the door and passed into the room, closing it behind him.

Inside, he halted and gazed around. Sir Arthur Playmer was seated behind a large oak desk, scrutinizing some X-ray prints. He looked up irritably as Red entered. Then, as he saw a stranger in the room, he laid the prints down and stood up. He was tall and thin — painfully so. He wore a morning coat and grey trousers with a fine pinstripe. His hair was grey and his neat moustache the same colour. His eyes were pale and piercing, and his nose and lips thin and precise-looking. His forehead — as would be expected of a man as intelligent as he — was wide and deep.

He looked at Red, who still stood nonchalantly near the door. 'I instructed my nurse that I was not to be disturbed,' he said, raising one eyebrow questioningly. His voice was as thin as the rest of him, clear and meticulous. He spoke perfectly.

Red nodded and began to cross towards a vacant chair. He sat in it and lit a cigarette. 'You must not lay the blame on your nurse, Sir Arthur,' he said. 'She did her best to stop me, short of physical violence. In addition to which, I informed her that I was a policeman.'

'Are you?'

'Not exactly. The name is Benton, Red Benton. I'm a private detective by profession.'

'I see. Then I can go ahead and ask my nurse to get in touch with the police, so that we can have you ejected, Mister Benton.'

'You can — but I don't think you will.'

Sir Arthur paused with his hand on the lever which would put him through to the reception room. 'Really? Why is that?'

'Because I am not here for a consultation. I am here because I believe that you can be of some assistance in solving a crime which has been committed. You are acknowledged as the greatest abdominal specialist in England, and a lot depends on that fact.'

The specialist sat down again. He leaned forward. 'You do interest me, Mister Benton. Please go on.'

'It's like this. I suppose you've read of

the bodies in the Thames? One found a while ago, a tramp; one found more recently, the daughter of Lord Spinnerton?'

'I have read of them, certainly. But from the papers I was led to believe that they were accidents.'

'That was what the police wished the public to believe. They thought that possibly it might lull the murderer into a false sense of security. But they weren't, Sir Arthur. The stomachs of those two corpses were cut open in rather a strange way. The police surgeon can see no reason for the cuts being inflicted as they were. I thought that you, being an eminent specialist, would possibly spot something which he had missed. I am convinced that the two crimes are connected, Sir Arthur, and I am convinced they were not the work of a madman. I have obtained permission for you to view this last body, and if you will do so I would be extremely pleased. I will, of course, pay your fee.'

Sir Arthur tapped his fingernails on his desk pensively. Then he smiled. 'Don't worry about the fee, Mister Benton. You know, I was just having a look at the X-ray plates of the Duchess of Lockinhead's abdominal bone structure. Not a very prepossessing photograph. In fact, it has bored me so much, that I rather think I would like to do something a little out of the ordinary, such as you suggest. And if I can help you to apprehend a murderer I will be extremely pleased. When is it possible for me to see the remains?'

Red stubbed his cigarette and smiled. 'I knew you'd help, Sir Arthur. And you can see the body any time you wish.'

'Excellent! I should like to see it right away, if you have no objections. I have no urgent appointments — only a matter of two calls to make on two clients, and since both of them are in perfect health, the calls can wait.' He smiled reflectively. 'You can thank your lucky stars you aren't a well-known specialist, Mister Benton,' he said. 'The number of rich people who are convinced they are suffering from everything from cancer to Bright's disease is really phenomenal. Yet, they are quite healthy. And I have to prescribe for them — minister to them — when actually they are healthier than I can ever hope to be. Ah me, it is indeed a most annoying state of affairs. And yet, Mister Benton, I am forced to take a grave view of their imaginary ailments, when actually I would prefer to tell them to go to the devil and do a bit of good hard work! What hypocrites money makes of us, does it not?'

While he had been speaking, the doctor had donned his coat and hat, taken an ivory headed stick from the rack, and was ready to go. 'Which morgue, Mister Benton?' he asked.

'Green Lane, Sir Arthur.'

'Good, good! We will walk there. It is only a matter of fifteen minutes, is it not, and it would be a waste of time to call my car. Added to which, Mister Benton, we can never do too much walking, if we wish to keep in condition. That is a bit of advice for which I will not charge you.' He smiled.

'It is also a bit of advice for which I would not pay you,' replied Red, smiling back. 'I always do a lot of walking.'

'And yet, Mister Benton, you would be

surprised if I told you how much I charge some of my clients for that same advice.'

They laughed and left the office. The nurse receptionist gazed at them with startled eyes as they passed.

'It's personality that does it, sugar,' smiled Red, and they went out leaving her gaping after them.

★ ★ ★

Sir Arthur Playmer mopped his brow with his handkerchief, rose, and stripped off the rubber gloves he had been wearing. He turned round to Red Benton after throwing the sheet back across the dead girl.

'Well?' said Red.

The specialist knitted his brows. 'I should say, Mister Benton, that the murderer could have conducted a thorough examination into her internal stomach organs.'

'You mean . . . ?'

'I mean that she was subjected to a close scrutiny for some reason; and although the water has obliterated a lot of useful signs, I would also say that her death occurred *prior* to the cuts and incisions being made. In fact, Mister Benton, from certain minute signs I would say that her entire stomach was *poisoned while she was still alive!* The incisions were made *after death had occurred!*'

3

When Red arrived back at his office he immediately sat down and picked up the telephone. He got his number in record time, and luckily Gregor proved to be on hand. 'Listen, Inspector — ' began Red.

'*Detective* Inspector,' growled Gregor from the other end.

Red grinned into the mouthpiece. 'All right, Detective Inspector then.'

'What are you calling about?' said Gregor. 'I'm busy.'

'I took Sir Arthur Playmer down to see the body . . . and he says that the stomach was poisoned and opened up after death. Can you get your surgeon to make a further and closer examination?'

'Naturally,' replied Gregor. 'Are you sure about this?'

'Dead sure. And by the way . . . when you get his report I'd like you to come along and see me — and bring the dossier on the tramp you found.'

'Who the hell d'you think I am, Benton? A page boy or something?'

'With those feet?' chuckled Red. 'Certainly not!'

'If you want to see the files you can come up to the Yard,' said the irritable detective inspector. 'I'll phone you after the divisional surgeon has made his second examination.'

'OK,' Red told him. 'If Mohammed can't get the mountain to come to him, I guess it's up to Mohammed to do the running round. Let me know when you're ready!' He hung up, sat back in his swivel chair, lit a cigarette, and pressed the desk button.

Happy Harringay materialized. He was wearing a loud check suit, an extremely flamboyant tie, and the inevitable black derby hat. He was holding between his teeth a large and evil-smelling cigar, an indispensable portion of his equipment.

Mister Harringay was American, and proud of it. The only bits of England which attracted him were the public houses where he could purchase Scotch Whisky. The only reason he tolerated life in England was because if he returned to the States, the Homicide Bureau might want to ask him some very awkward questions about a dead gangster who owed his corpse-like condition entirely to Mister Harringay's ministrations. He was Red's assistant and, although all solid bone from the neck up, he was a handy man with his 'betsy', as he affectionately called his revolver.

'Yeah, Borss?' he enquired curiously.

'Got a spot of work for you, Happy,' Red informed him. A dismal expression crossed Happy's features. It wasn't that he was lazy — it was simply that a spot of work might interfere with his whisky-imbibing activities. 'I want you to make some enquiries for me in the public houses along a certain section of the Thames.'

Happy's dolorous expression vanished, to be replaced with an interested look. He leaned forward over the desk and gave his whole and undivided attention to his employer.

'Be careful,' Red told him. 'Of course, it's only a routine matter and may not throw any light on anything. You'll find the lowest type of pubs you can, and try to contact some of the criminal characters you'll probably find in them. Then, when you get friendly with them, make discreet enquiries — ask them if there's been any funny business going on around those parts . . . you know the kind of stuff; you've done it before.'

'Sure,' said Happy, all smiles. 'Leave it to me, Borss. That ain't work, goin' in bar-rooms! That's pleasure!'

Red gave him expense money and full directions, and Happy took his leave. Shortly afterwards, Red left the office himself and took a cab to Berkeley Square where Lord Spinnerton had his town house. Red pressed the door bell and waited.

A rotund butler opened the door and eyed Red's travel-stained raincoat and seedy trilby with evident displeasure. 'Tradesmen's entrance round the back, if you please,' he said fruitily.

'Is that so, Algernon?' said Red, not amused. 'Well for your information, I am not the Fuller brush man. Now get your

136

dogs moving and inform his Lordship that Mister Benton of Benton Investigations waits without. And,' added Red, 'in view of the fact that I am not accustomed to waiting without, I'll step inside.'

The butler gave him a haughty look and allowed him to enter.

Red stood idly by the door, flicking cigarette ash onto the expensive hall carpet, until the portly butler returned. There was more respect evident in his tone now.

'His Lordship desires me to say that he will be delighted to receive you, sir. Will you walk this way . . . ?'

Lord Spinnerton hastened across to greet Red as he entered the old oak-paneled library. Lines of worry and distress were etched into his forehead; his daughter's untimely death had seemingly hit him very hard. He was a typical English aristocrat, even to a monocle in his eye. As Red nodded in greeting, he said: 'Mister Benton! Have you some news — have you found who murdered Dalia?'

Red shook his head. 'That'll take time, Lord Spinnerton. These cases can't be cracked open on the spur of the moment. I've only been working on the case a short time, but I have already found out a great deal. The reason I came here is, I'm in search of some information. I thought that you might be able to tell me exactly what your daughter did on the night of the murder. Where she went, who she went with, and all that.'

Spinnerton shook his head. 'I'm afraid I can't help you much there, Mister Benton. All I know is that she went to some night club with a young man called Staples — she had been keeping company with him for some time. Apparently, while they were walking home, there was a slight quarrel — nothing of importance, Staples says — but Dalia flounced off in a temper, saying she would see herself home. After which, young Staples went straight to his flat and knew nothing until I telephoned him the following day to ask what had become of Dalia.'

'So she was missing the entire night before she was found in the river?'

'Yes. I didn't call the police, because she very often sleeps with friends.'

'Friends?' said Red, sharply. 'What kind of friends?'

An angry look spread over Lord Spinnerton's face. 'Lady friends of hers, Mister Benton,' he said. 'I trust you did not place any other construction on my words?'

'I place no constructions on anything until it's made perfectly clear to me, Lord Spinnerton. I merely ask because had she spent the night with a gentleman friend it might explain much.'

'There was nothing of that nature,' said his Lordship. 'Dalia was a very clean-living girl. She had a few boyfriends, of course. But they were all of good character and family.'

'I see. Perhaps you could give me the address of the young man with whom she spent the evening preceding her disappearance?'

'I think so.' Lord Spinnerton opened a drawer of the desk and rummaged among the contents. He rose again, holding a visiting card; this he handed to Red. 'Ronald Staples, Flat 306, Durbank Mansions, Elm Tree Road, St. Johns Wood, London, N.W.8', it read, and the detective slipped it inside his own card case.

'Thank you,' he said. 'I think I will call on this young man.'

'I fear you will not find anything there,' said Spinnerton. 'He is an upright and honorable young fellow and has already made a full statement to the police.'

'Who knows,' Red told him enigmatically, and moved towards the door. 'Good day, Lord Spinnerton.'

'Good day, Mister Benton. You will let me know if anything happens, I take it?'

'Of course.'

The stout butler escorted Red to the door and let him out. Red walked down the drive and found the taxi he had left waiting. He stepped in and gave Staples's address. The taxi rolled away towards St. Johns Wood.

It drew up outside an imposing block of flats and Red climbed out, told the driver to wait again, then entered the door. To the right was an automatic lift; he pressed the button and watched the lift descend. He stepped in and pressed the 'up' button for the fourth floor.

Staples's flat was almost facing the doors of the lift and Red played a tune on the electric bell. The door opened and a young, well-groomed, dark-haired man of about twenty-four, dressed in slippers and dressing gown, glanced out. He looked rather surprised to see Red.

'Mister Staples?' asked the detective.

'Er — yes, I'm Staples.'

'Good. I'm working on the Spinnerton case. I'd like to ask you a few questions if I may.'

A surly expression crossed the young man's face. He scowled. 'Damn it all! How much longer are you policemen going to keep bothering me with your questions?'

A steely glint entered Red's eyes. He pushed against the man's chest with his right hand, forced him backwards into the flat and followed him in. He slammed the flat door. Staples had gone pale with anger under the rough treatment, and his fists were clenched tightly. He looked as if he would hit out at any moment.

'I wouldn't!' cautioned Red. 'It might be very painful for you if you start to get tough.'

'What right have you to come here and handle me like this?' choked Staples passionately.

'There's a woman been murdered,' Red told him icily. 'But you don't seem to be very worried about that! However, if, by answering a few more questions you can throw any light on the matter, I will see that you answer them!'

Staples suddenly cooled off, threw open a door on the right and beckoned Red in. Red entered and made himself at home on a luxurious divan.

'Sorry,' Staples said. 'I'm a bit over-wrought, you know. I lost my temper.'

Red's cold expression did not change. He lit a cigarette and flicked the match into the firegrate. 'I understand you were with Dalia Spinnerton shortly before she vanished?' he said.

Staples nodded. 'We went to the Silver Slipper night club and had dinner together.'

'How was it you walked home? It's a long way from the Silver Slipper to Berkeley Square.'

'The truth was that Dalia got rather

. . . well . . . tight. She'd had quite a lot to drink and I thought the fresh air might clear her head a bit. You see, I didn't want her to go home in that condition. Lord Spinnerton had rather a good opinion of me, and I wouldn't have cared for him to lose it.'

'How did you separate?'

Staples flushed. 'We quarrelled. Dalia insisted that she wanted to go into a gambling club . . . but I can't tell you where it is. You're a detective, and quite a number of my friends go there. They wouldn't thank me if I gave away the location of the place to the police.'

'You can tell me,' said Red, handing the young man one of his cards. 'I'm not attached to the official police. I've been retained by Lord Spinnerton.'

Staples seemed satisfied. 'Well,' he said, 'it's run each night in a disused warehouse basement at the bottom of Churls Alley. Dalia wanted to go on there, but I was tired and wanted to go home. There was the dickens of a row, then she simply left me standing, and I was so angry I didn't bother to follow her.'

'It sounds rather fantastic to believe that, no matter how annoyed you were, you allowed a girl you were fond of to go wandering around a low quarter of the city, drunk and alone.'

'Who said I was fond of her?' interjected Staples. 'That's a lie! I liked her — she was good company — but she had too many chaps hanging round her for my liking.'

'I see. She was fond of the opposite sex?'

'Definitely. But I am sure that none of her male friends were responsible for killing her. They were all feather-headed young fools.'

'You can never tell,' said Red. He rose from his seat and picked up his hat. 'Thank you for the information, Mister Staples. It has been most enlightening. If I wish to know anything more I will pay you another visit.'

When Red returned to the office he sat for a long time in thought. Then the phone rang and he picked it up. It was Gregor.

'Can you come round now? The

surgeon has made his examination and Playmer was right about the cause of death being poison.'

Within ten minutes a cab decanted Red at the entrance to the Yard. A constable showed him to Gregor's office. That worthy was seated at his desk with a thin dossier in front of him. He was regarding a piece of paper intently, but as Red came in he laid it aside.

'So the stomach was poisoned?' said Benton.

Gregor nodded. 'It seems that as far as can be ascertained, the cuts were inflicted as Playmer says — after death. The surgeon says that after a more careful examination he has detected the presence of some poison in the stomach. Only an infinitesimal amount; I suppose the effect of the water has more-or-less ruined some of the more visible traces. The funny thing is that we can't affirm what type of poison it is. It's an unknown quantity to us.'

4

'Did you bring the dossier on the tramp up from the files?' demanded Red.

Gregor threw the slim folder towards him and Red picked it up and opened it.

'There wasn't very much to put on the record,' Gregor explained. 'We knew nothing about the chap — couldn't find anyone who'd identify him. We published a description in the papers, but it didn't tally with any missing persons.'

Red studied the coroner's report and findings, and the medical report. He thumbed down the text rapidly, but suddenly he stopped and looked up at Gregor. 'Says here that the tramp was suffering from cancer of the stomach. The cancer was not active when the body was discovered, although it had been a malignant growth and had obviously been worsening for some time.'

'What does that have to do with anything?' asked Gregor.

'Doesn't it strike you that since Playmer says the stomach was cut open to make an examination possible, whoever cut the stomach open did so for the purpose of observing the development of the cancer?'

'It does not,' demurred Gregor. 'How could anyone know the man was suffering from cancer? And what sense would there be in examining it in any case? Besides that, Dalia Spinnerton was not infected with cancer — she was perfectly healthy.'

'That's so,' admitted Red. 'At the same time it's a point worth noting. Now I wonder if this body had any poison in the stomach which was missed at the post-mortem?'

'We'd have to disinter the body to find out.'

'Do you intend to do so?'

Gregor shrugged. 'If the cause of death has been mistaken I think we better had. Do you think yourself that it will have any bearing on the case? It's a damned nasty job, Benton!'

'Dig it up,' said Red slowly. 'We'd better know just what we're up against. If there is evidence of the same type of unknown poison in the body of the tramp as there was in the girl's well, we'll at least be certain that both murders are tied up in some strange way.'

Gregor nodded. He said: 'This case is the very devil! How can the murder of a cheap tramp possibly be tied up with the murder of a society girl? What motive could cover two people so widely separated in their spheres?'

'That,' said Red, 'is what we are going to find out! You know, Inspector, I am beginning to get rather interested in this case. I've an idea that there is more in it than meets the eye!' He picked up his hat from the desk, selected a photograph from the dossier and stuck it in his pocket. It was a photograph of the dead man, and he was careful not to let the detective inspector see him remove it.

Gregor, who had been sitting with his back to Red, staring from the window, now swung round again. 'Going?'

'I am. I'll get in touch with you if anything important crops up — but I have a feeling we're a long, long way off solving this business just yet.'

'I have a feeling we'll never solve it.'

'Tut, tut, Inspector.'

'Detective Inspector,' rumbled Gregor.

Red smiled. 'Don't get discouraged,' he told the rattled Gregor. 'I've never fallen down on a case yet.'

'No? Well, there always has to be a first time, Benton. Don't be so sure of yourself.'

'So long, Inspector!'

'*Detecti* — oh, what's the use,' groaned Gregor. Red smiled in a saintly fashion. The door closed behind him. When he had gone, Gregor made arrangements to have the body of the tramp disinterred.

Back at the office, Red found Happy Harringay awaiting him. With Happy — who was looking extremely happy indeed — was a small, shifty individual with a peculiar, ragged monstrosity of a cap and a semi-leer painted permanently upon his stubble-covered features.

'This is 'Shorty,' Borss,' Happy informed his employer radiantly.

'I can see how he got the name,' agreed Red. 'But what's he sellin'?'

He of the ragged cap touched same

furtively, and wiped his lips and nose on the back of his jacket sleeve. ''ere,' he said. 'This 'ere bloke wot's wiv me sez as 'ow you ain't no nark fer th' bobbies — is that right, Boss?'

'That's right,' agreed Red. 'I'm a private detective — no connection 'wiv' the 'bobbies' whatsoever. Why?'

The small character sniffled. 'I'm careful, see? Don't do fer the likes o' me ter get mixed up wiv th' rozzers. But if you ain't a two-piece copper, an' you'll gi'me five quid like this 'ere bloke tells me, then, I can do you a favour.'

'Out with it,' said Red. 'If it's worth it you'll get ten quid. What is it you know?'

'It's like this. This bloke comes inter the pub wot he patronizes, an' starts abuyin' whisky. Gets ter talkin' wiv me abaht the bloke wot was done in wot they found in the water a while back. Now, has h'it so 'appens, I noo' that cove! We uster meet reg'lar dahn at the pub an' discust the Parlihamentery sit'huhation. Only this night 'e ses 'as 'ow 'e's fixed up to do a job fer a swell. This swell's agoin' ter give 'im free pahnd fer 'elpin' 'im, but 'e don't know what the job is 'till 'e sees this feller wot's payin' 'im! Unnerstan'?'

'Just about,' said Red. 'Go on.'

'Well, I h'ask 'im 'oo the 'ell the bloke is wot's given 'im the job, but 'e says 'e can't tell me, but 'e's meetin' 'im ahtside the pub. Sure enough h'out 'e goes soon arter, an' bein' curious by nacher, h'out I goes arter 'im. W'en I gets ahtside 'e's already walkin' away with this 'ere bloke towards Churls Alley. I can't make out the other bloke proper wet wiv me bad eyes an' all, but 'e's a swell orlright an' dressed up fit ter kill in real proper clothes. 'e was abaht six foot tall an' skinny-like, an' 'e was walkin' at a good rate o' knots.'

'And you never saw your friend after that?'

'Not a blurry 'ide not 'air of 'im! Till I saw in the papers after 'ow 'e'd bin fished aht of the river.'

'How d'you know it was your friend?'

'By the description an' the tail wot 'e 'ad tatthood on 'is arm. 'e useter go ter sea wiv me, an' we both 'ad wun done in Bombay. Look 'ere!' He of the unprepossessing face rolled back his tattered sleeve and displayed a hula girl on his arm. Beneath was the name Lulu.

Red ferreted in his pocket and brought out the photograph of the dead man which he had filched from the records. He held it up in front of the furtive gentleman. 'Is this him?'

'That's 'im! That's 'arry! Cripes! Don't 'e look blurry awful!'

Red grinned. 'He would. He'd been in the river quite a bit when this was taken. Harry, you said his name was?'

''arry, that's it. 'e never seemed ter know wot his secon' name was 'isself.'

'Did he have any family?'

'Not that 'e ever spoke of.'

Red fished a note from his wallet and handed it to the man. The friend of 'arry seemed displeased by this action.

'Wot th' 'ell!' he exploded. 'This is a ten poun' note!'

'Isn't that what you wanted?'

'Nark it, guvnor! D'yer want me run in? If I tried ter parss this 'ere I'd 'ave arf o' Scotland Yard arter me afore I 'ad time ter turn rahnd!'

Red grinned, selected ten one-pound

notes and handed him those.

'That's more like h'it,' said the man. 'Crikey, it's bin a bit of orlright meetin' h'up wiv your pal 'ere.'

'Go back to your pub,' Red told him. 'And keep your ears open. If you hear of anything which concerns the girl who was found dead there a day or so ago, let me know and there's another ten for you!'

'I will, guvnor, swelp me I will!'

'And give my assistant your name and address before you go in case I wish to get in touch with you again.'

'Ain't got no address — name's 'erbert 'emmings. Yer can find me dahn at the Blue Goat almost hennny time, guv'nor.'

'Why didn't you go forward and identify your pal in answer to the police appeal?' said Red.

'Wot! No bloomin' fear! Told you, I don't wanter get mixed up wiv the ruddy flatties! Not 'erbert 'emmings! Besides, they would'n 'ave gi'e no ten quid for it, would they?'

Happy escorted him out, leaving Red wearing a wide grin.

5

Red Benton turned out of his apartments, walked east a few blocks and turned in at his offices. It was 11.30 the following day, and Red had not long risen. He found Happy Harringay waiting for him in the office.

'Been a phone call for you, Borss,' said Happy from behind the tumbler of whisky he was demolishing. 'Guy called — lemme see ... Playfair? Nope. Playboy?'

'Playmer? Sir Arthur Playmer?'

'Sure, that's the Playmer all right, all right! He called about an hour back.'

'Leave any message?'

'Yeah. Says for you to call him when you got in.'

Red entered the inner office, slung his hat neatly on to a peg and slung his raincoat over a chair back. He lunged into the swivel chair, picked up the phone, and gave his number.

'Sir Arthur Playmer's surgery,' came the voice of the nurse.

'Is that you, honey?' grinned Red. 'Put me on to the big noise!'

'Hello? Who's that speaking? Is it George?'

'No, it isn't George. Maybe you've forgotten me already? Was round at the surgery a little while ago . . . Benton's the name.'

'Oh, Mister Benton,' sniffed the nurse. 'Yes — Sir Arthur is expecting a call from you, I believe. Hold on — I'll put you through to him.'

Red lit a cigarette while he waited. Then Sir Arthur Playmer's thin, precise voice came over the wire. 'Mister Benton?'

'Sure. You left word for me to contact you — did you find any fresh angle on the killing?'

'No, it wasn't anything important really. I just wanted to know how you're getting on with the case — naturally, having examined the body, I'm interested.'

'Naturally. Well I found out one or two things more. Such as the fact that the tramp who was bumped off in the same

155

way as the Spinnerton doll had cancer in the guts. Does that convey anything to you?'

There was a pause at the other end of the phone. 'It would seem to imply that the man was cut open in order that he could be inspected.'

'That's how I figured it — but then, the Dalia dame didn't have any cancer, so how do you tie that up with things?'

The specialist laughed. 'It isn't my job to tie it up with things, Mister Benton. That is your affair. If I can assist you in any way, though . . . '

'Yes, I know, I'll get in touch with you. Thanks a lot.' Red slid the receiver back on to the hooks. He took out the photograph of the dead tramp and studied it hard. Then he shrugged and slid it back into his pocket.

The thought uppermost in his mind was the gambling den in Churls Alley. Someone should go around there and look it over — someone who wouldn't rouse suspicion. But who? A woman would be the best bet. That was another stumbling block. Red didn't know any young females who would care to enter into a thing of this nature. Unless . . .

He picked up the phone again and dialled Playmer's number. He heard the voice of the nurse. 'It's that man again,' he told her. 'Benton. It's important.'

'Very well, Mister Benton; I'll put you through to Sir Arthur . . . '

'Skip it! It's *you* I want.'

'What on earth do you mean, Mister Benton . . . ?'

'Let that wait,' said Red. 'I thought maybe you'd like to help.'

'Help?'

'Sure, help track down a criminal. There won't be any danger in it for you.'

'But I don't understand.'

'Meet me at the corner of Harley St. for lunch and I'll explain things to you then.'

'Are you sure this isn't a joke?'

'Cross my heart,' said Red earnestly. 'Murder's no joke.'

'Very well then. I don't know what you're driving at, but I'll meet you at one thirty — that's my lunch period. And your story had better be good!'

'Rely on it!' said Red and slammed down the phone. He thought for a minute, then thumbed through the London telephone directory and found Ronald Staple's number. He dialled that. Staples came on the wire; he sounded tired and lazy, as if he'd spent a bad night.

'This gambling den you told me about — where you used to go with Dalia — is it still open?'

'Of course!' Staples sounded surprised. 'I was there only last night myself. I'm beginning to think the games are as crooked as hell though. Why?'

'How does anyone get in?'

'You have to have a friend to vouch for you in the first place. Once you have been inside they issue you with a green card. Then, in future, all you have to do is knock, show the card, and you're in.'

'I guess a lot of people get there, huh? What I mean is, the doorman wouldn't be likely to know every member by sight?'

'I should hardly think so.'

'Do the cards have names on them?'

'Naturally.'

'Such as?'

'Mine just has R. Staples, that's all. What's all this leading up to, Mister Benton?'

'I'll tell you when I see you,' Red smiled.

'But when will I see you?'

'In about fifteen minutes. I'm on my way round now.'

★ ★ ★

The pretty young nurse from Sir Arthur Playmer's office was waiting at the specified spot when Red, having borrowed Staples's club card, arrived. Red coolly linked her arm through his and steered her to the nearest café. He made no move to open the conversation until she had eaten lunch. Then, when they were both sitting back over cigarettes and good coffee, he said: 'I'm glad you came along, Miss . . . ?'

'Sheila Tarrant,' she told him. She flicked ash into the ash tray and looked at him from clear, level eyes. 'Exactly what is it you want, Mister Benton?'

'Call me Red, Sheila,' grinned the detective; and so infectious was his grin, that she felt no offence at what, in others, would have been almost impertinence.

'All right — Red,' she smiled. 'And now that you've put the whole affair on such a friendly footing, why did you ask to meet me?'

'Well, Sheila, not for the usual reason a fellow wants to meet a girl. I thought that you might like to help.'

'Help? Elucidate, Red.'

Quickly and plainly, Red told her exactly what had happened up to the minute. When he had finished she was silent, lost in thought. 'I don't understand. How can I help?'

'Quite simple. I want someone to go down to this gambling den in Churls Alley to sit in on the games, keep their ears open and note anything which is said and which might have a bearing on the case. I want you to get talking to someone down there who was in the place the night Dalia Spinnerton was murdered — see if she ever got as far as the den that night — and if so, what time she left. You may not find out anything — but dressed in the right clothes, and with a hundred pounds or so to gamble with, you'd easily pass for one of those featherbrained society dames. You know the type I mean — Dalia Spinnerton was one of them — and you could make your enquiries as if you were one of her friends who was curious about her. You certainly wouldn't attract as much suspicion as I or my assistant Happy would. It shouldn't be hard for you to act the dumb debutante.'

'Thank you!'

'Don't get me wrong. I'm asking you to do this job because I reckon, from your looks, you're a pretty smart young lady. I'll give you two hundred pounds — rig yourself out with some classy duds, hire a mink wrap, and use what's left to gamble with. Will you take the job on?'

'I've always wanted to help a detective!'

'Swell! You're a sport, Sheila — in the nicest sense of the word! I've seen girls like you before — but only in my dreams!'

'Flatterer,' smiled Sheila. 'But how do I go about getting in?'

'That's easy — knock on the door and use this card.' He gave her the green card and she examined it curiously. 'It says R. Staples on it.'

'Sure. It belongs to a guy I know. But don't worry about that. They can't keep a photograph of all their clients, and as far as they are concerned your name is Roberta Staples. Do this job for me and it's worth another hundred if you pick up any useful information. Added to that, you can keep the clothes you buy.'

'I won't want the hundred, Red. I'll be perfectly satisfied to just hang on to the outfit I buy with this money.'

'Atta girl. But just the same, if you do pick up any facts it'll be worth the money to me — so you'd better not refuse the offer of the extra hundred before you have done the job. I'll send Happy along with you, and he can wait in the Alley while you go on in. You'll like Happy — he'll probably have a bottle of Scotch with him, but don't let that upset you. It has no more effect on him than a dose of cough mixture. He'll look after you going to the club and coming back — it isn't a very nice neighborhood for unescorted ladies.'

Sheila looked at him for some seconds. Slowly a smile formed on her lips. She said: 'You know, Red, I don't know why I'm being foolish enough to stick my neck into all this! If it were anyone else but you who had asked me I'd have called the nearest policeman. Yet, simply because of the way you talk, and smile, and act, here I am practically ready to do anything you want me to! I can't understand myself! Instead of being frightened, or perplexed, I'm actually awfully intrigued — and flattered that you should have chosen me to help you!'

Red took her hand which lay on the tablecloth. He pressed it tightly, looking deep into her eyes. 'I asked you because you seemed the type of girl I like a lot,' he told her. 'Because I knew you were sensible enough to realize that I wasn't fooling about this business; that you could really do a lot of good — maybe. I think I knew what your answer would be — and I wasn't wrong. I'll send Happy round to pick you up at about ten o'clock. And good luck, honey!'

* * *

'So that's it, Happy. You pick the girl up at the address I gave you, take her to Churls Alley, and wait outside for her. And mind you wait — if anything happens to the kid I'll make you wish you'd never met up with me, see!'

'Don't worry, Borss! You know me! She'll be as safe as if she was wid one of them shapper-hones.' Mister Harringay clapped on his derby and left. When he had been gone about ten minutes, Red rested his chin on his hands and thought hard. He was wondering if he had been quite right in asking Sheila to take the risk.

Not that there was very much risk attached to the affair — after all, Happy was with her. Red would have gone himself, but that shock of red hair of his, those thin features, were things which were well known to members of the underworld. His presence might have given the game away if he had been seen.

A sudden decision to follow on — to shadow the girl and Happy, just in case, formed in his mind. He got up and reached for his hat.

'Mister Benton?'

The voice came from the direction of the doorway and it was a coarse, uneducated voice. Red turned easily and eyed the owner. The man standing there was about thirty-five to forty years of age. He wore a blue serge suit; no coat; a dark, wide Stetson type of trilby; a neat, blue striped shirt; and blue tie. His face was brutal-looking and pugnacious, but it was the man's size which shook Red. Red himself was quite tall, but this man towered over him and made him feel like a pygmy. He had hands like hams, hanging from arms akin to young tree trunks. His muscles bulged under his tight-fitting jacket; his shoulders filled the doorway.

'I'm Benton. If you're wanting to hire me for some job, you're too late. Got too much on hand — and anyway, it's after hours.'

The man strode forward and threw a thick bundle on the desk. Red picked it up and flicked it. It was a bundle of Bank of England five-pound notes.

'Five hundred pounds,' said the stranger. 'That's my offer for your services.'

'What do you want doing?'

'I want you to come along with me, that's all.'

'That's all, is it? And where do you want me to go?'

'To my place outside town. It's this way. There's a guy who's blackmailing me. Has been for years. Means to keep it up. But I'm not playing any longer. Going to report the matter to the police. Want a witness to hide behind the curtains. Listen to what he says when he comes. Step out and hold him up while I call the Yard. Five hundred pounds is a lot of dough. Hear you've got a cash-register mind. Take it or leave it. Plenty other private coppers be glad to do the job for me for that money.'

'I'll *take* the job — I'll *leave* the dough.'

'I don't get you.'

Red crossed to a wall safe, spun the combination deftly, popped the money in the safe and swung the door shut. 'That's in case you're lying. At least you won't get the money back.'

'Why — you — '

'Let's go,' said Red. He slipped a revolver from his desk and into his pocket. He put his hat on and pulled down the brim.

'My car's outside,' said the stranger.

They went down the stairs and along the hall. Outside in the darkness was a long, low car. They climbed in.

'What's your name?' said Red.

'Harvey — if it matters. Gerald Harvey.'

'Your business?'

'That's none of your business. You do the job I'm paying you for, that's all.'

The car swung out into the main road. They made good time through London's traffic. They passed into the suburbs and down long, lonely lanes. The stranger pulled the car up suddenly. Red was cautious; the whole set-up smelled to him. He'd just gone along for the ride and to see where it would lead — if it tied up with anything . . .

But he wasn't cautious enough. He knew that the second he felt something hard and round jabbing into his side.

'Get out!'

He got out. The stranger followed, menacing him with the revolver he had produced. Red made a furtive reach for his own gun. The stranger lashed him savagely across the wrist with the muzzle of the weapon he held. 'You're going too far, Benton. I was told to tell you that and give you a foretaste of what's coming to you if you don't cry off the Spinnerton shemozzle. We'll let you live this time — but if I have to see you again . . . '

'So the story about blackmail was phoney?'

The stranger laughed. 'Sure, smart dick! Fancy you being taken for a sap like that!' His tone changed, becoming venomous. 'You'll only get this one chance, Benton. This is your first and last warning — understand?'

Red made no reply.

'Understand?' snarled the tall man again.

'Aren't you outgrowing your strength?' queried Red calmly.

'You still trying to act smart? Well, I'll alter that. After you've had a taste of what's coming your way, you won't feel so peppy. You'll learn to keep your nose clean, Mister Benton!'

'And if I don't?'

'*This*!' snapped the man. He reversed the gun rapidly and lashed out at Red's jaw. The hard, metallic butt connected, cracking against the side of Red's cheek. Red felt a couple of teeth cave in and was aware of sharp, fierce pangs of agony running up the side of his face. Then the revolver smashed home again on his right ear, and he went down.

The landscape went spinning round, round, round, faster, faster, and then jumbled together in a mad, kaleidoscopic whirl of grey tones. He shot downwards into a bottomless, inky black void . . .

6

Red came up out of the black pit he was in; slowly, slowly, the darkness dissipated. The jet black gave way to a grey, then to a light golden colour; the gold swooped together into a big, brassy-looking disk which whirled round dizzily before his eyes. The disc gradually resolved itself into a fleshy circle, and vaguer shapes surrounding it became distinguishable. Round and round whirled the circle, slower, slower yet. It became a spinning, moon-like face whirling with its surroundings.

Red made a supreme effort. The room stopped spinning, and the face clicked into place before him . . .

'Are you all right, Benton?' It was the voice and face of Detective Inspector Gregor. He was seated in a chair, facing Red, who was lying back on a low bench.

Red licked his dry lips and felt his sore, numbed jaw.

'You're lucky,' said Gregor. 'Your jaw isn't smashed; just a few teeth gone.'

Red groaned and tried to sit up. Dizziness overcame him again and he sank back.

'What happened?' queried Gregor. 'They picked you up well out of town and brought you to the local station, here. They found a photograph which had obviously been taken from the records at the Yard in your pocket. So they sent for me.'

'That's right,' Red rumbled. 'The one of the tramp — I took it while you weren't looking, Inspector.'

'That's what you think,' grinned Gregor. 'I watched you take it — but I thought that if it would help us solve anything, well, why should I bother to stop you? But, just the same, I could see you all the time through the window I was looking out of — we policemen aren't so dumb, Benton.'

Red smiled feebly and accepted the glass of water which a moustached sergeant held out to him. After he had sipped it he felt a little better; well enough to tell Gregor what had occurred. He did. When he was through, Gregor shook his head sadly.

'I can't understand you, Benton. You're mad! You go batting around without any clear idea of where you're going or what you're heading into. If you don't get results from one angle you try another and another until you do get results — or a wham on the head!'

Red managed a grin. 'That's the way I like it, Inspector. The guy who hit me tonight was a hit too fast for me — but I'll know him next time I see him.'

'But you might have known it was a frame-up.'

'I did. But I hoped I'd be smarter than them, that's all. And I wasn't.'

Gregor regarded the laceration in the centre of the blue bruises on Benton's jaw, and nodded. 'You certainly weren't,' he agreed.

Red tried to sit up again, fought the spell of nausea which gripped him, and swung his legs from the bench. 'Maybe I wasn't,' he admitted. 'But the game isn't played out yet, Gregor. This is only the first innings — and in the last innings I always bowl them out!'

Gregor pursed his lips dubiously, and smiled pityingly. 'You know, one of these days . . . '

'I'm going to be a bit too clever! I know, Inspector, you told me before. Where are we?'

'A little place about ten miles outside London. I've got one of the squad cars outside, so if you'd like a lift back?'

'I would, thanks. What's the time?'

'Pretty late,' said Gregor, glancing at his watch. 'Turned two o'clock in the morning.'

Red whistled and stood up, feeling a lot better. The detective inspector joined him and they left the small station. Outside waited a patrol car, and in less than fifteen minutes they were drawing into the deserted London streets. The car took Red directly to his apartments and he alighted, somewhat unsteadily.

'So long, Benton,' called Gregor, leaning out of the car. 'And for the love of Mike, stay as far away from trouble as you can!'

The car turned away, slid up the dark streets, and vanished from sight. Red stroked his jaw tenderly, fumbled for his key and let himself into his apartments. He took the automatic lift to his own floor.

He went into the bathroom, filled the bowl with icy water, then plunged his head into it. The fuzziness left his brain, and he dried his face, found some sticking plaster and decorated his jaw with two cross strips. He found the whisky and soda, poured himself out a half tumbler full, and swallowed it. The fire of it in his throat and belly warmed him. He went into the sitting room, slumped into an armchair by the phone, and called up his office. There was no reply. He wondered if Happy and the girl would return to the office or to his apartment.

He didn't have to wonder for long. Even as the thought crossed his mind, the door opened and Happy came in. 'There you are,' said Red. 'I've been wondering — how'd you get on?'

Happy seemed agitated, worried. He suddenly removed his derby and pointed

174

to a large lump on his skull near the ear. 'I got slugged while I was coming home with the dame,' he said.

Red was on his feet instantly. 'Where is she?' he barked.

'I don' know, Borss. When I came round she wasn't there!'

7

Red flopped back into the chair. He indicated the whisky decanter and Happy poured himself a good four fingers and drained it off. He sat down opposite Red and rubbed his skull at the back.

'O.K. Happy — let's hear the rest of it.'

'There ain't no rest of it, Borss. She'd just come outta the joint and we was walkin' along the street when someone lifts me lid offa me head from behind. I am about to turn round and ask them why they do this when, socko! I stops a heavy blunt weapon wid the back of my neck. I goes out like a light, only twice as quick, and as I goes down I hears the skirt scream . . . the next thing I know I am lyin' in the gutter feelin' mighty sore. I gets up an' rushes around an' about lookin' for the dame, but it is no use — she has taken the air, but fast. So I comes on right back here.'

'Did she tell you anything that she

found out in the club?'

'Nope, not a thing. We was only together about five minutes when I got bopped over the turnip.'

Red stood up and looked down at Happy. 'I've a notion to sock you again,' he stated harshly. 'You big hunk of no-damned-good! I told you to watch out for any funny stuff!'

Mister Harringay looked embarrassed and went a dull red shade. 'I don't see it, Borss. How did they know the dame was down there spyin' on them? You an' me an' her was the only guys what knew about it!'

Red shook his head. He himself, he reflected, had not been much brighter than Happy, to take that ride with the large gentleman. They had both been whammed upon the brainbox. 'That's all you know? You saw no one hanging round there?'

Happy shook his head.

'We can't play this thing alone any-more,' stated Red, reaching for the phone. 'The girl's gone and it's my fault. I should never have sent her down there at all. Anyhow, I'll have to get the cops in on it now. They'll have to bust up that club and investigate . . . I don't reckon it'll do a whole lot of good, but it's the only thing to do right now!'

He made his call quickly to Gregor, and was lucky enough to contact him immediately.

'I was just replacing that photograph in the files,' said Gregor irritably. 'This is a hell of a time to call me, Benton. Three in the morning!'

'Forget the time,' Red told him. 'Maybe it'll help you, too, if I inform you that assault and battery and kidnapping have been going on in this man's city . . . and I'm responsible for it!'

'How'd you mean, Benton, you're responsible?'

Red told him.

'Hell!' exploded Gregor. 'Why did you keep this dark until now? Where is this gambling club?'

'It's an all-night stand at the bottom of Churls Alley so far as I can make out — maybe I can come along with you if you're going to raid the place?'

'Sure! I'll get a couple of squad cars

out and pick you up on the way down. You'd better bring along that stupid assistant of yours to show us exactly where is where!'

Gregor rung off, and Red lit a cigarette, took a drink of whisky and motioned to Happy. They left the building and walked down the road to the corner. In five minutes two radio cars came tearing along, halted to pick them up, and shot on into the night towards the dock areas.

'Here it is,' said Happy eventually. 'Down this side road here.'

The driver pulled up as silently as possible, and Gregor, Red, Happy, and half a dozen men tumbled from the two cars.

They traversed a deserted, narrow alley and came to the door at the end of it. Gregor rapped imperatively upon it. A small grill shot open and a bearded face peered out at them.

'Open up,' snapped Gregor. 'It's the police!'

The mouth belonging to the face gave a gasp; the grill swung shut sharply, and there was a sound of retreating footsteps in the passage beyond.

'It's only a light door,' rapped Gregor. 'Break it in!'

Two burly policemen put their shoulders to the door and pushed. There was a dismal creaking; the door crashed inwards, hanging from one hinge. The forces of the law poured into the old warehouse.

At the end of the short passage they burst into a brilliantly lighted room which appeared to be in some confusion. Green baize gaming tables were being hastily laid away beneath some uprooted floorboards. Men were dashing about bearing roulette wheels and similar devices. A number of people in evening dress were jostling about at an exit on the far side of the room.

But as the police burst in, the bustle stopped and the excitement died away.

'Who's running this place?' barked Gregor.

A short, dark man stepped forward. 'I am.'

'And who are you?'

'The name is Gibson, officer. Daniel Gibson. I use this place to entertain my friends.'

'So I see,' agreed Gregor, pointing towards a stack of notes and counters on one of the tables. 'And your entertainment tax comes pretty high, huh?'

Gibson shrugged. 'You know how it is, Inspector. A man has to make a living. Even you policemen must find it difficult to make ends meet . . . now if I were to . . . ' He held out a wad of notes, totalling about five hundred pounds, to the inspector.

The frown which crossed Gregor's features would have made more sensitive men than Gibson totter on their feet. But apparently Gibson was not very sensitive.

'Daniel in the lion's den,' grinned Red to Gregor.

'Daniel'll be in another kind of den before the night's out,' grunted the plump detective inspector. 'Daniel doesn't know it yet but he just put his head into the lion's mouth! And this is one time the lion's teeth are going to meet in Daniel's neck!' He scowled at the dark man. 'What makes you think English police officers can be bribed?'

'Can't they?' said Gibson in surprise.

'My mistake! I only arrived from America a few months ago — I wasn't sure, but it was worth a try. At least there's no harm done.'

'You're dead wrong there,' Red pointed out. 'Over here they'll take a very, very serious view of attempting to bribe a policeman. It'll be one more charge for you to answer!'

'Take this skunk out of here,' yapped Gregor, and two constables led the luckless Gibson away.

'Now what?' demanded Red, after names and addresses had been taken, and a number of arrests made. 'What do you propose to do about the girl?'

Gregor shrugged. 'What can we do? Only question these people and organise a search of the district.'

'Why, you chump,' bawled Red. 'That girl may be getting killed while you're doing that. If any of these folks do know anything, do you expect them to spill it?'

'What else can we do? We can only question them!'

'Third-degree them! Nothing like a length of rubber hose for making a guy talk. Some of them *must* have seen Sheila in here and noticed what she did, who she talked to. It's up to you to make them tell if you have to beat it out of them!'

'Take it easy, Benton! You can't get away with that rough stuff over this side.'

'But it's justifiable in this case!'

'It's *never* justifiable! Not in any case. You're the smart boy who got her into the jam — why don't you get her out, clever pants?'

Red cooled off somewhat. 'I guess you're right, I did get her into it — and I'll never rest if the kid gets hurt. If she does, by God, I'll kill the murderous rat who's doing all this, myself!'

'And land yourself in a heap of trouble? Talk sense, Benton!'

Red grunted, turned, and followed by Happy, swung away towards the exit.

'Where the devil are you going now?' called Gregor.

'To take a look around myself — you coppers wouldn't see anything if it was served up on a dinner plate with parsley in front of your silly noses!'

Red vanished, and Gregor smiled. It

was obvious that for once Red Benton was extremely rattled. He knew he had got the girl into the mess and he doubted his capability for getting her out. For just once in his life, Red Benton wasn't sure of himself.

*　*　*

Red and Happy arrived home, tired and worn, at six o'clock the same morning. They had wandered the dark and narrow streets of dockland and searched the wharves and the shadows of the gaunt, grim warehouses all night. The only thing they had found was the cute hat which Sheila had been wearing when she had set out upon her mission. Red slumped wearily into a chair, dangled the hat on his finger and shook his head.

'It's no use, Happy. I'm licked. I might as well admit it! I haven't got the foggiest notion of where to start looking. All we can do is hope the girl isn't too badly treated — maybe we'll get a line to follow later on . . . '

Happy heaved a dolorous sigh. He felt

more responsible than did Red for what had happened.

Gradually weariness overcame their troubled minds, and in a few minutes Happy's head fell back and loud snores emerged from his unlovely lips. Red blinked. He wanted to stay awake, to think, but he was dead tired. In another five minutes he had followed Mister Harringay's example.

The clock struck seven, eight, nine, ten.

Red awoke with a start and glanced at the clock. He shook Happy, but that worthy snored on. He took one of Happy's ears and tugged. Mister Harringay mumbled a swear word.

'Ten thirty,' Red told him. 'Get washed and dressed and meet me down at the office at once!'

'Sure!'

It was a pleasant morning, and Red felt that he would like to walk down to the office to clear his head. His jaw was stiff and numb where it had been hit, and he was compelled to talk from the side of his mouth. His ear also had been burst, and smarted like the devil. He hoped the eardrum had not been injured: he was aware that he could not hear through the injured organ as yet, but that had happened after a smack on the ear with a revolver. If all was well his hearing would return in good time.

He turned into the office, passing the caretaker on his way. 'There be a gent waiting for you up there, Mister Benton,' the caretaker told him. 'Toff, he is. He arrived about five minutes since and asked me what time you would be down here. I told him you generally arrived about this time and he said he'd wait.'

'Thanks, Jackson.'

The visitor was none other than Sir Arthur Playmer. He wore his usual morning attire and a worried frown. He carried a rolled umbrella beneath one arm, and as Red arrived he laid this on the desk and stood up. 'My God, Mister Benton,' he said in a strained voice. 'This is horrible, horrible!'

'You've heard?'

'Yes, Inspector Gregor rung me up to tell me. Of course I don't blame you for sending the poor child down there; you weren't to know that anything like this would happen.'

'I'm hoping it won't be so bad,' Red told him.

There was a knock at the outer office door. Red went through, opened it, and admitted a uniformed man holding a large Gladstone bag.

'Yes?'

'You name of Benton?'

'That's it.'

'Sign here, please.'

'Hold on,' said Red. 'What's all this?' He indicated the bag which the man had set down inside the office.

'Package for you, sir.'

Red touched it with his foot. He had had packages like this one before. Once, one had contained a time bomb. He turned to the carrier. 'Where'd you get this — and from whom?'

'Gentleman brought it into the office this morning, sir. Gave the name of Smith and said he wanted it delivering express.'

'Where are you from?'

'Bolton's carriage services, sir.'

'Hmm!' Red signed the slip and the

messenger touched his cap and retired. Red picked up the bag warily, shook it, and held it to his ear. There were no suspicious sounds. He carried it into the inner office and Playmer looked at it curiously.

'Just delivered,' explained Red 'The devil of it is, I don't know what's in it. May be a mistake.' He looked at the label pasted on the side. It was no mistake. There was his name and address, plainly enough. He unsnapped the straps which held it and tried to turn the lock. It was fast.

'Locked,' he told Playmer.

'Does it matter so much?' said the agitated specialist. 'I mean, couldn't you leave it until we decide what's to be done about Sheila . . . ?'

'No — it may have a bearing on the case. I've had evidence from anonymous persons delivered to me like this before. We'll try it.' He inserted a thin master key in the lock, failed to open the bag, and tried a more likely one. This time the lock clicked. He snapped the bag open, and the contents were revealed . . .

His hands clenched convulsively. Sir Arthur turned white and turned away with a hoarse gasp. Red took a pull at himself and picked up a scrap of paper which was pinned to the thing inside the bag. He read it out in a low tone: 'This is for you, Benton. For you and for Playmer and for that nosey detective inspector and for anyone else who sticks their snoot into my business, including your thick-skulled assistant. Lay off, Benton, or else!'

Red dropped the note on the desk, raced through the office, and down the stairs. The carter was just climbing into his van.

'What kind of man gave that bag in?' panted Red.

The carter scratched his head. 'Big he was, and broad. Real ugly, too, but well dressed.'

Red nodded. 'I thought so — the same monkey who smacked me down last night. Stick around, brother,' he told the carter. 'You'll be needed for questioning when the police get here.'

He went up the stairs again, taking them two at a time. He went into the

189

office. Playmer was sitting down, pale but composed. He was used to sights such as what the Gladstone bag had revealed. A surgeon has to be. Red phoned the Yard again and got through. Gregor was there once more. Red said: 'Get over here, Inspector — just had a present of Sheila's head in a bag — cut off at the neck!'

'I thought you might have,' said Gregor. He didn't seem very surprised. His next remark explained why. 'We just found the trunk, minus the head, floating down the river. The stomach was cut like the other two were.'

8

At nine o'clock that night, Red, with Happy accompanying him, left the office, making his way to Churls Alley. There was a quarter moon out, giving sufficient radiance to see fairly well, and at the corner of the alley Red pressed back into the shadows on one side, Happy remaining on the opposite side. In the distance a clock chimed twelve. Red stamped and blew his hands. In spite of the fact that it was a reasonably warm evening, he felt cold through standing there, motionless.

One chimed out, and then two. A constable on his beat passed by, and Red hugged the shadows to avoid answering awkward questions.

At about half past two, the sound of footsteps echoing down the road roused Red from his reverie. He tried to pierce the gloom with his eyes to see if Happy was on the alert, but it was pitch-black on that side. He tensed and waited. His heart jumped as a tall, broad man came into sight. The moonlight revealed him as the stranger who had taken Red for a ride the previous night.

He paused near the alley and glanced furtively about him. His eyes scanned the length of the road and noted it was deserted. Reassured, he made to stride out again.

From the shadows where Happy was hiding came a loud and unlovely snore!

It echoed down the silent street, seeming to Red as loud as the last trump. The hefty merchant gave a visible start, then stared hard into the shadows. Red could see his face in the moonlight; could see the alarm and indecision written on it. Then the man changed his mind and began to return the way he had come.

Red came out of the shadows and started running towards him before he could get a start. The man whirled, spotted the detective, and snarled as he recognised him. Then his right hand streaked inside his coat pocket and came out levelling a wicked revolver. His fingers tightened on the trigger.

At that very moment, Happy, having been awakened by the noise of Red's running feet, managed to grasp the situation immediately and stepped from the shadows, bringing his clubbed gun down on the tall man's head. The tall man buckled at the knees, twisted, and dropped to the street. His hat fell off and his head cracked against the curb.

No words passed between Happy and Red. They hoisted the tall man between them and carried him through the squalid streets until they reached the main road. They flagged a taxi, dumped him in, and sang 'Sweet Adeline' to give the cabby the impression that they were under the influence.

They got him up to Red's apartment and dumped him in a chair. Red bathed his head with cold water and forced brandy between his lips.

'Geez!' commented Happy suddenly. 'I remember this guy now! He is a punk which is called Cyclone Harry back in the States on account of he busts many joints up, and when he is through they look like a cyclone has hit them! Only, he bumps off Van Scabolli and the coppers put the heat on, and he had to skip town about two, three years back.'

'You don't say? So he's a regular American gunman?'

'Yeah, this is the mug all right. Is this the herb which hit you over the noggin, Borss?'

'It is.'

Cyclone Harry stirred and groaned. Red slopped cold water over his face and forced more brandy between his lips. The big man's eyes flickered open. He tried to raise his arms, but discovered that they were firmly roped to the chair he was in.

'Hello Harry!' said Red genially.

Harry stared at him. 'Benton! I thought there was something fishy around that alleyway when I heard that snore. So it was you, you goddamned copper!'

'It was. We wanted to see you urgently, Harry. Just to ask you a few questions, you know.'

Yeah? Well save your breath! I ain't answering nothing! The guy I work for pays me well, see, and you runts can't pin a thing on me! You won't find out a thing!'

'No? I figure you'll talk under the third degree, Harry.'

Cyclone Harry sneered. 'Can it, copper! There ain't no third degree in this country — the coppers are all nice little gentlemen who wouldn't say boo to a turkey.'

'Who said a thing about the coppers?' asked Red. He crossed the room and returned carrying a small electric fire with half a dozen long elements across the front of it. He plugged it in and watched the elements until they glowed red hot. Harry watched, also, with distended eyes.

Happy guzzled whisky contentedly.

'Take this lug's shoes an' socks off, Happy,' Red told him.

'Geeze, Borss, that'll spoil me whisky!'

'Take 'em off! You can drink later.'

Mournfully, Happy put aside the whisky and attended to the job of removing Harry's neat sports shoes. Red stood by and watched, every now and then glancing at the fire.

'What — what you goin' to do, Benton?' It was a dry croak which forced itself from Harry's lips. His eyes were apprehensively glued to the glowing electric fire.

'You know, Cyclone,' Red told him, staring thoughtfully into the fire, 'I don't like guys like you. I will take the greatest delight in toasting your feet on this contraption — the only thing which might persuade me to lay off would be a little information . . .'

Unable to speak, Harry shook his head dumbly. Happy returned to his whisky, paying no attention to the scene.

'I hoped I'd see you around there tonight,' Red told the Cyclone. 'And I was lucky! What's wrong, Cyclone?' he enquired as Harry shook visibly. 'Yellow?'

Cyclone made no reply.

'You weren't so yellow when you smacked me with that gun, were you? You were OK when you carried that poor kid's head into the carriage office and addressed it to me!' He picked up one of Harry's feet and held it towards the fire. 'Talking?' he demanded. Harry wriggled frantically but still shook his head.

With a sudden, quick movement, Red drove the foot onto the red hot bars. There was the sizzling and hissing of flesh and a bubbling scream tore from Harry's thick lips. His features twisted in agony. The sickly-sweet stench of burnt flesh filled the room and Happy put his whisky down in disgust.

'Talking yet, Harry?'

The Cyclone sobbed convulsively, but his lips remained closed. Red brought the foot down onto the bars again.

'Christ!' shrieked Harry. 'I'll talk! I'll spill it! Don't — '

The shot came from the doorway, shattering the light bulb and leaving Happy and Red momentarily blinded. The butt of a revolver smashed home on Happy's skull and he went down, the whisky glass tinkling to the floor beside him. In the glow from the fire, Red saw a dark figure sliding over the room towards him. A knee jarred into his groin, and as he gasped and doubled up a pair of hands gripped his throat, squeezing.

The hands came away, leaving Red blue in the face, gasping for breath. A knife sliced through the bonds holding Cyclone. He came from the chair, limping on his burned foot. He made for Red.

'No time for that,' hissed a soft voice. 'Come on!'

'He shouldn't have done that,' mumbled Harry. 'He shouldn't have burned me! I'll strangle him . . . '

He was coming for Red, murder in his eyes, his hands glimmering weirdly in the fireglow. Red felt a spark of fear rushing up his spine, a spark which galvanized him into action. He reached for the fire and gripped the corner of the metal. He heaved it upwards and forwards into Harry's face.

A scream of unbearable agony burst from the Cyclone's throat. It swelled and bubbled round the room, reaching a crescendo, dying away and then starting again. The fire, on falling to the floor, had shorted and gone out.

'I'm blind!' screamed Harry. 'I'm blind . . . ' He was scrabbling at his inflamed, raw face, screaming. Red saw the dark figure grab him by the arm and lead him towards the door.

'I can't see! I've got to get to the hospital,' sobbed Harry. 'I can't come with you.'

'Do you think I'll leave you here to tell all you know, you fool?' hissed the intruder.

Harry was resisting his pulling, and the intruder suddenly saw Red rising from the floor. He stepped out into the hallway, drew a revolver, and fired three times — once at Harry, twice at Red.

Harry's shrieks suddenly ceased. He folded up like a broken doll and slumped to the floor. Red had ducked when he saw the gun drawn and the bullets whistled over him harmlessly.

Then the intruder was gone, and Red felt in no state to follow.

9

Red crossed dizzily to the table lamp and switched it on. By its shaded light he gazed round the room of death.

Harry was lying crumpled up, his legs bent beneath him, his face staring sightlessly upwards. Although the skin on his features was red and blistered from contact with the fire, his suffering was over. Harry was dead. A neat, round hole in his forehead testified mutely to that.

Happy was lying beside the wall, his head resting in a pool of his beloved whisky. From the hair roots at the top of his brow, a thin trickle of blood was oozing down from over his pudgy nose and past the corner of his open mouth.

Red hoisted him to the settee and flopped him down there. He brought a damp cloth and laid it across Mister Harringay's head. He then dragged Cyclone Harry over to the wall and threw a rug across him, concealing the scorched, agonized face.

He turned to the mirror, examining his own features. They were purple and swollen; there was a blue bruise round his throat where the killer had gripped and strangled. He found it hurt him to swallow. He poured out some raw whisky and drank it neat. Then he took some whisky over to Happy and forced it between that unconscious gentleman's lips.

A figure suddenly appeared in the open doorway, and Red started up, thinking the murderer had returned. When he spotted the thin form of Sir Arthur Playmer, he relaxed and sank into a chair.

The specialist came into the room, his eyes taking in the details of the scene unbelievingly. 'Benton! What . . . how . . . ?'

'Just a little dress rehearsal,' sighed Red. 'I'm glad to see you, Sir Arthur. You can phone Gregor and tell him I've got one of the men he wants here — a guy called Cyclone Harry.'

'You have? Why, that's wonderful! Perhaps we can get him to tell us whatever he knows.'

Red shook his head and indicated the rug. The specialist went over to it moved it aside, shuddering as he saw the scorched face. He knelt by the dead man.

'He's dead all right,' he said, rising. 'What on earth's been happening? I'd been out on an emergency case — Lady Astra had an attack of acute appendicitis. I packed her off to hospital, and since it was rather stuffy in the sick room I thought it would do me good to walk home. I was passing here when I heard shots!'

'You did. But did you see anyone dodge out past you as you came in?'

'Why, no. I pressed the button for the lift, but the top door must have been open, because it didn't come down. I started walking, and as I got to the second floor I heard the lift going down past me. Do you actually mean to say that the man who is behind all this was in that lift?'

'That is so — will you put that call through?'

'Of course, of course.'

'I'll be telling Gregor what happened here so if you wish to hear you'll have to wait — I couldn't find the energy to tell the story twice.'

Sir Arthur nodded, picked up the phone and put through the call. While he did so, Red walked out into the passage and took a look round. He saw something there which interested him greatly.

'Gregor isn't at the Yard,' said Sir Arthur as he returned.

'Ask them to get in touch with him — it's urgent.'

Sir Arthur did so, and received an assurance that the Yard would communicate with the detective inspector immediately. He put the phone down and began to revive Happy.

'Did you recognize the killer?' asked the specialist as Red drained another whisky.

Red shook his head.

'What happened to that man's face?' shuddered the specialist, pointing to Cyclone Harry.

'I seem to recollect his running it up against the electric fire,' Red told him quietly. 'That, of course, was after he'd warmed his feet up — or rather, after we warmed them up for him.'

'You — you warmed them up for him? I don't quite understand.'

'You'll hear it all when Gregor gets here, Sir Arthur.'

Happy, under the ministrations of the surgeon, gave a prodigious yawn and came back to his senses. His first action was to reach for the whisky bottle; his second to put the neck to his mouth and drink deeply. Then he deigned to glance about him.

Red heard the sound of a car drawing up outside. He said: 'Gregor, or I miss my guess! Won't he be wild about being dragged from his warm bed at this hour.'

There were heavy feet on the stairs and Gregor appeared in the doorway. He barked: 'They called me, got me up, told me you wanted me here urgently. It'd better be good, Benton! What is it?'

'It is good, Inspector . . . it's under the rug.'

Gregor looked, and cursed. 'He's dead!'

'He'd be a marvel if he wasn't, Inspector,' smiled Red.

'Who burnt his puss and his feet like that?' snapped Gregor.

'I don't know. Someone must have been giving him matches to play with.'

'Now look here, Benton. It seems to me this man's been tortured! It wouldn't have been your idea to do that, in order to get information out of him . . . would it?'

'How clever of you to guess, Inspector.'

'So it was you? I suppose you know you can get into pretty bad trouble for doing a thing like that?'

'Baloney!' snorted Red. 'You coppers are always chucking your weight about — in the wrong direction! As far as you're concerned, the guy was coming for me to kill me off, and I had to protect myself, so I slung the fire at him.'

'Yeah? And it hit him in the face and then fell onto the soles of his feet and burnt them also — him having very thoughtfully removed his shoes and socks for the purpose! Tell another, Benton!'

'Forget it! Self-defence, call it — which it was. Why don't you concentrate on catching the criminal instead of shooting your trap off?'

'I suppose you're going to tell me he was here?'

'That's about the size of it. He was. Who'd you think shot this sap — me?'

'I wouldn't put it past you,' grunted Gregor.

'No? Then where's the gun, smart guy?'

Gregor crossed to the settee and picked up a thirty-two from there. 'Fired recently,' he stated, examining it. 'Three chambers used. I wouldn't be surprised if this was it, Benton!'

'Where the hell did that come from?' gasped Red.

'I wonder!' Gregor was feeling sarcastic. 'Maybe a little fairy dropped it!'

'Maybe so,' agreed Red. 'And another little fairy picked it up! A loud mouthed, flat-footed fairy!'

Gregor's scowl was positively awesome, but it had no visible effect on Red. He said: 'Give over, Inspector! Quit jumping to conclusions and let me give you the drift of what really happened.'

10

When Sir Arthur had taken his leave and Gregor had departed with the corpse in an ambulance, Red roamed into the kitchen, from whence came a steady gurgling sound. He found Happy glued to the rim of a glass containing whisky, and he joined him in a drink. The wound on his assistant's head was not serious, but the amount of whisky Happy had imbibed on top of it, was. When they made their way to the other room, Happy was lurching like a ship in a storm.

'Well,' said Red, 'somehow I don't think you'll be able to crawl back to your billet tonight, Happy.'

Happy agreed. He had rooms about three streets away from Red's but he was in no condition to walk two yards unsupported.

'You'd better sleep it off here,' Red told him. 'I'll fix up the bunk bed for you.'

The two detectives did not rise until

well on into the afternoon. Then they partook of a light meal, and Happy drank more Scotch. Red was constantly amazed at Mister Harringay's capability for packing whisky away. The man was like a giant distillery — Red was sure his liver must be resembling a sieve by this time.

They took it easy, reading the papers, not having anything in particular to do. There was no line to be followed at the moment. But Red had high hopes that something would turn up before long. He was not mistaken, for at nine o'clock that evening, or thereabouts, the telephone shrilled.

Red laid aside his magazine and answered it. The thin, precise tones of Sir Arthur Playmer became audible. 'Mister Benton?'

'Talking.'

'Thank Heavens! I had hoped it would be you — I was afraid you might have gone out on a case.'

'You had something important?'

'Very much so! Mister Benton, I am stepping into the matter again. I believe I know where this killer we are seeking has his headquarters.'

'What?' Red sat up, rigid.

'I was talking to a patient of mine today, down at the cancer clinic — we give them free treatment, you know, the people who can't afford to pay. We — er — try different methods of treatment on them. This man was a night watchman from the opposite side of the river to Churls Alley. He claims to have seen dark figures sneaking into Potters Warehouse.'

'Potters Warehouse?'

'Yes — I didn't know where that was until he explained. It seems that the gambling den which was closed was Gillams Warehouse. Next to it, adjoining it, is Potters Warehouse, which used to be a store-place for sacks of grain but has long been closed down. As a matter of fact, the second floor of Potters actually runs over the first floor of Gillams.'

'I see. The Gillam place is quite a small warehouse, and only has one small floor. You mean that this Potters Warehouse occupies half the space on the second floor?'

'That's it, Mister Benton. And this

patient of mine claims to have seen men entering Potters Warehouse, which has been closed for a long time. He thought nothing of it until I mentioned the murders to him, then he recalled what he had seen.'

'But I understand that the police have been over those places?'

'That's why I don't want to communicate with the police, until I know if there really is something to the man's tale. I'd feel a fool if there wasn't — but I feel we ought to take a further look round ourselves. What do you say?'

'I think perhaps you're right,' Red replied thoughtfully. 'Yes. You are right!'

'Good. Now I thought that if we did find anything, we could keep an eye on the place and one of us could telephone your assistant and tell him to get the police.'

'Yes, we could. I'll tell him to stand by the phone,' Red agreed. 'Where are you?'

'I'm at my surgery, but I'll meet you near the end of Churls Alley in, say, half an hour.'

'Fine. I'll see you there.' Red hung up.

He collected his gun and made certain it was fully loaded and operating correctly. He gave Happy his instructions, impressing them firmly on his mind. Then he left.

Sir Arthur was already waiting for him, a dark coat and hat on. Red said: 'In case of trouble, have you a revolver?'

'I have. It hasn't been used for a long time but I loaded it specially and it should be all right.'

'Let's make sure,' Red told him. Sir Arthur slid a small .32 into his hand and Red looked it over carefully. It was fairly dark and he had to rely mainly on his sense of touch. Finally, he shot the magazine into place and returned it. 'Seems all right,' he said. 'Nice and free. Shall we go?'

Sir Arthur led the way and they traversed the street in the opposite direction to Churls Alley. After a walk of a hundred yards they reached another narrow opening.

'Salters Alley,' explained Sir Arthur. 'We get to Potters Warehouse down here.'

This entry was not a dead end. It led out onto an old, disused wharf. Rotting woodwork and moss-covered walls gave sure signs that nothing had been unloaded into Potters Warehouse for many years. Sir Arthur began to move along by the wall, searchingly. He came to a wooden door set into the stonework.

He tried it and crouched back as it swung open. 'It's not locked!'

Red made no reply. He was on the alert, ready for any eventuality. They passed on into a damp, musty-smelling room. On the right was the dividing wall which cut off Potters from Gillams, which had been the gambling den.

On the left, a flight of wooden stairs ran upwards into the shadows. Red ran his torch round the walls warily. Sir Arthur started for the steps. They went up, slowly, carefully, treading as softly as possible. They reached the store-room above.

This was twice the size of the room below, since it also extended above Gillams Warehouse. Over on the right were stacked some smouldering sacks of grain. Apart from this there was nothing.

The dust had been disturbed. Red assumed that that was because the police had been abroad, stamping up and down with large, flat feet. Then he remembered something else, something very important. It was that in the warehouse wall which fronted on Churls Alley, there was a door, high up, from which the sacks of grain had once been loaded onto lorries by means of a pulley block. But there was no sign of this door on the right-hand wall up here. Could it be behind the sacks of grain?

He went over to the grain, pulled the two end sacks aside, and saw the edge of the door. So it was there!

'Move the rest of the sacks and go right on in!'

It was Sir Arthur who had spoken, but his voice was changed. It was harsh, unreal . . . Red turned slowly and stood outlined in the glare of the other man's torch. Sir Arthur had taken his revolver from his pocket and levelled it at Red. 'Put your torch down — do as I say!'

Red put up no argument. He dropped his torch and began to move the sacks from the door. He said: 'If I walk out here I'll fall twenty feet and probably break something! Is that the big idea?'

'Not at all. You're perfectly safe — for now. There is a smaller dispatch room beyond that door. They used to keep the grain which was ready to go out in there.'

Red opened the door, which was unlocked, and went in. Sir Arthur was on his heels. He switched on a light by the doorway, and a green shaded lamp in the centre of the room cast a brilliant whiteness on the paraphernalia which was scattered about. There were test tubes, retorts, burners, and over on a small bench a complete kit of surgical tools. Under the lamp was a straight-backed chair, and over the wooden arms of this, straps were looped. In one corner was a white porcelain operating table. A surgeon's white theater smock was hanging from the wall, and from the small tin bowl in one corner a pair of rubber gloves protruded.

Red whistled and sat down on the bench by the surgical equipment. He could now see the door on the right, which opened out twenty-odd feet above Churls Alley. 'A pretty set-up, Sir Arthur.'

'It satisfies me, and is sufficient for my needs.'

'Am I to understand by all this that you are the killer of Sheila Tarrant?'

'You are. And also of the nameless tramp, Dalia Spinnerton, and Cyclone Harry, who was my assistant.'

'And shortly you will be adding me to your already excellent score?'

'That, to put it bluntly, is the rough idea, Mister Benton. I had not intended to, but if you wish . . . ?'

'Oh, I do, Sir Arthur, I most certainly do!'

'Very well. Mister Benton. You are unaware of the fact, but I have only one month to live — perhaps a little longer. Not much. I have been examined by one of my contemporaries and he vouches for it — I myself know it is true. I am suffering from cancer of the stomach, Mister Benton — not a pleasant complaint, assure you. Yet there is a chance for me! When I found this out I was experimenting with a new serum down at the cancer research centre. I was, of course, conducting my experiments on vermin — rats and guinea pigs. But the serum was far from perfected, for although it killed the cancer, shortly afterwards the subject also died. The serum was too strong for the rats' stomachs — but was it too strong for the human stomach? I knew that the serum was merely in its experimental stages and was almost certain to kill anyone it was used on; therefore I could not experiment on human subjects down at the centre. With my own death drawing painfully near, I was desperate. I enlisted the aid of Cyclone Harry, who came to me one night with a bullet in his intestines. He had been shot while breaking into a large store, shot by the watchman, and naturally he was anxious for his wound to be kept dark from the police. He was in great pain and offered me much money to remove the bullet and patch him up without notifying the authorities. The money was of little consequence — I have already a great amount of my own — but I thought that if I did him this service I could blackmail him into helping me to accomplish the idea I had in mind.'

'And it worked?' asked Red.

'It worked excellently, Mister Benton. The operation was a ticklish one, but Harry pulled through. Then I had him in my power, and gave him his instructions. My first task was to get a cancer sufferer. While I was waiting for this, Harry looked around and found this place, which was ideal for my purpose. Piece by piece, at night, we imported our equipment until we were all ready. Then I located a tramp, a homeless street wanderer, a man whom nobody would miss. He was attending the centre for treatment for a cancer of the stomach and was ideal for my purpose. I spoke to him one night in a public house; told him I had a job for him. I met him the night after, took him down to Churls Alley, and told him to wait with Cyclone, who would tell him what to do. Then I came here the way we have just come and opened the door over there, which looks out into Churls Alley. Meanwhile, Cyclone had knocked the man unconscious, and when I lowered a rope he tied him to it and I hauled him up.

'I won't bother you with details of my

experiments. They went on for some days — injections into the stomach, until eventually the growth was no longer active — was, in fact, entirely dead. I had to operate on the man to ascertain exactly what effect the serum had had, and under the operation he died. I was not sure whether his demise was due to the serum, the stress of events, or the operation. Certainly the stomach was poisoned, but there was the chance that he might have lived. So I had to find a fresh subject, and Harry threw the tramp into the river. We waited a long time for another human guinea pig. This time we had no need of an actual cancer sufferer — I merely wished to see if the serum itself was capable of killing an adult human being. At last our chance came, and we caught a young lady, very drunk, going to the gambling den. We treated her in the same way as the tramp. I injected the serum. She died! The serum killed her. I performed a second post mortem to see exactly which organs the serum had affected. Then we disposed of the body and I set to work each night to perfect the serum — you must remember that my time was growing short, Mister Benton, and life is very sweet! The rest you can probably guess.'

'I can,' said Red quietly. 'Then I asked you to look the second corpse over; it was a fine chance for you to run with the hare and hunt with the hounds, so you took it. But when I called your nurse, Sheila Tarrant, and told her she could help me with the case, you were listening on the extension line. And when you saw her down there with Happy, you decided I was getting too warm!'

'Just so! So that when she left the club, my excellent friend, Cyclone Harry, knocked your assistant unconscious. Then he hit the girl and we hauled her up here by means of the rope. I was not quite ready, but I tried the altered serum on her. It killed again. I thought it was time you had a warning. Of course, Cyclone had already given you one warning earlier that night, but I fancied that if you received a more gruesome sign it would be more effective.'

'And you cut off the kid's head and got

Cyclone to send it!'

'Right, Mister Benton; I cried off the case myself, hoping you would follow suit, but I had misjudged you! Instead of being afraid, you became more determined! Last night, when you saw Cyclone near Churls Alley, he was waiting for a further victim for my experiments. For I now think the serum is perfect! We had hoped to catch the police constable who controls that portion of the docks, but your interference prevented this. I had the door in Churls Alley slightly open and I looked down on the whole affair. I followed you to your apartment and reached it just as Cyclone was about to confess.'

'Then, after you had intervened — ' said Red, ' — after you had shot Harry, you were worried in case he wasn't quite dead. Also, you had an idea you might have been seen, and you wished to find out so that if you had, you could kill me before I spilled the beans. When you saw that everything was all right for you, you parked the gun on the settee to confuse the issue, knowing we would think the killer had thrown it there — but I suspected you by that time, Playmer!'

'You what? How could you have suspected me? I was most careful!'

'You made slips. In the first place, your story about having been out on a case was very flimsy. I made enquiries today and found there was no such person as Lady Astra. Then, you said that while you were coming up the stairs the lift was going down. But when, after your arrival, I looked in the passage, the lift was still at the top. Since there had been no time for anyone else to have used it, you must have been lying about it going down. In all probability you went no further than the end of the passage, then you returned.'

'Very clever, Mister Benton. Go on.'

'Tonight, when you phoned, I was still more suspicious. But I wished to be absolutely certain. So when you let me look over your revolver in the roadway, I *unloaded* it before I gave it back to you! How do you like that, Sir Arthur?'

Sir Arthur Playmer gaped at his useless revolver and pulled the trigger. It clicked weakly. Then he shifted his eyes to Red, who was still seated nonchalantly on the bench, but who now held a forty-five in a businesslike fashion. 'I had no intention of being experiment number four,' Red told him.

'But why didn't you inform the police?' gasped the murderer.

Red slowly allowed his revolver to drop, and looked Sir Arthur in the eye. 'Have you ever heard that I happen to have a cash-register mind?'

A gleam of hope entered Playmer's eyes. He nodded. 'You mean . . . ?'

'Have you your cheque book on you?'

'I haven't, but . . . '

'Never mind. I took the trouble to find out who your bankers were and to obtain an uncrossed cheque on your bank. Here it is. And if you will be good enough to fill in five thousand pounds and your name, I will allow you to make your getaway — taking your serum with you.'

Sir Arthur looked at him. 'You give me your word of honour?'

'Naturally.'

'I trust you, Benton, Give me the

cheque!' He fumbled with his fountain pen, filled in the cheque, and handed it to Red.

Red smiled and tucked it in his pocket. 'Thank you, Sir Arthur. This covers my trouble very nicely. And now we can wait.'

'Wait? What for?'

'The police. You see, I did *not* order Happy to stand by the phone until he heard from me. I ordered him to trail us — Happy is a very good man at shadowing people — and when he had ascertained where we went, to go and bring the police. That gave me time to pull off this little deal with you. I'm a sucker for dough, Sir Arthur!'

'You swine, Benton! You gave me your word of honour!'

'So I did. Very wrong of me! But you don't think for one minute I'd keep it, after what you did to Sheila and the others, you rat . . . besides, a detective's word of honour isn't exactly his bond — not when dealing with a skunk like you! This will teach you never to trust a private sleuth, Sir Arthur. Not that you'll be worrying about that though, when you're dangling on the end of a rope with a nice, tight noose round your neck.'

Unexpectedly, Sir Arthur moved. His hand flashed up and flicked off the light switch. He hurled himself towards Red, who was momentarily taken off guard. The force of the collision knocked the gun from Red's hand, and as he grasped the surgeon, he felt him reaching over to the bench, reaching for a weapon . . .

A lancing pain tore down the sinews of the hand which was gripping Playmer's throat; the surgeon had secured a lancet from the bench. Red felt it coming for his face and eyes and hurled himself away.

The door opening on to Churls Alley was swung back. The specialist was throwing down a length of rope, obviously meaning to scramble down and escape by means of this. Red flung himself forward and caught Playmer's ankles in a Rugby tackle. He fought his way to his feet and clung on grimly; panting fiercely, they struggled and swayed on the very edge of the doorway. Twenty feet below them, dim starlight shone on Churls Alley. Then it happened!

Locked together they plunged over and smashed down onto the hard cobbles below . . .

★ ★ ★

'You were lucky, Benton,' growled Gregor. 'When we found you, you were lying on Playmer!'

'Oh yes,' grinned Red. 'How was the dear chap?'

'They won't be hanging him — his neck was broken. But if you hadn't landed on top of him, yours might have been in the same condition!'

Red smiled.

Gregor grunted. 'Well, you've done it again! I suppose you'll collect a wad of money from Lord Spinnerton?'

'A cool thousand over and above his retainer,' Red confessed, adjusting his tie.

'Is that where you're dashing off to now? Can't you wait to get your hands on the money? You should be resting up — you lost a lot of blood from that arm of yours.'

'I can't rest up — it's imperative that I

should be on the steps when the bank opens.'

'Why?'

'I have a cheque,' chuckled Red. 'For five thousand pounds! And I wish to cash it before the bank discovers that the man who drew it up for me is deceased.'

'What skullduggery have you been up to now?'

'Wouldn't you like to know, Inspector,' said Red with a gentle smile. 'But you'll just have to guess!'

'Detective Inspector,' grunted Gregor.

'Have it your way, Inspector,' grinned Red. 'Come on, Happy!'

The door closed behind Red and Happy. Detective Inspector Gregor heard them going down the stairs. Red was whistling 'We're in the money.'

THE END